Rapture of the Deep

David A. Grindberg

IndianGrass Books

Rapture of the Deep

Copyright © 2014 David A. Grindberg

All rights reserved.

COVER PHOTO: Copyright MoreAltitude 2014
COVER DESIGN: Lori Daniel
INTERIOR LAYOUT: Debbi Stocco

All rights reserved. No portion of this publication may be reproduced or utilized in any form or by any means, electronic or mechanical, including photocopying, without permission in writing from the publisher.

Inquiries should be addressed to: David A. Grindberg via IndianGrass Books

This is strictly a work of fiction. All characters, events, businesses, agencies, or organizations, are strictly a product of the author's imagination. Miner's State Park, Eldo's Pond and the town of Lake Pulaski, are merely backdrops. Any resemblance to actual people or events is purely coincidental.

Library of Congress Catalog Card Number: 2014905855

ISBN: 978-0-9916597-0-8, paperback
ISBN: 978-0-9916597-1-5, hardcover
ISBN: 978-0-9916597-2-2, ebook

Printed in the USA

Acknowledgments

Self-publishing is an oxymoron. From research to writing, editing to marketing, design to printing this has been a collaborative venture. My name is on the cover, but there is nothing "self" about its writing, production, and publication. I wish to thank the following people:

Self-Publishing Advisor—Carey Bligard

Research Resources—Ray Fiedler, Amy Donahe, Mark Thompson, Diane Sprague, and Dean Getting

Line Editor—Brad Edwards

Content Editors—Anne Kersten and Carey Bligard

Test Readers—Tammi Secor, Jim Wold, and Kent Westphal

Cover Photo— Copyright MoreAltitude 2014

Cover Designer—Lori Daniel

Interior Layout Designer—Debbi Stocco

There are, of course, many people who believe in this project. Chief among them are my children, Christian, Ashley, Karine, Jared, Kjerstin, Karianna, and especially Jill, my wife. Without Jill's love, encouragement, and patient understanding, *Rapture of the Deep* would never have come to fruition. It is to her that I dedicate this book.

"From birth, man carries the weight of gravity on his shoulders. He is bolted to earth, but man has only to sink beneath the surface and he is free."

Jacques Yves Cousteau

Chapter 1

Nothing.
    No light. No dark.
        No sound. No silence.
    Nothing.
        Time is suspended.
            Dreams are not remembered.

THE UNIVERSE COLLAPSES INTO ITSELF, and the space it occupies is so full that nothing enters. Nothing leaves. It is an impenetrable fog, formed yet formless, shell-like yet lacking discernable boundaries. It is an inviting womb cradling a mother's first love. This nothing cannot be achieved or possessed. Like gentle rain interrupting a mid summer's drought, it simply happens and when it does, it brings with it perfect repose.

Such is her slumber, night's deepest and her first, in weeks. Oh yes, she has tried. For days on end, she has tried. On her side, she has laid and watched as the clock dutifully checked away the minutes. She has poured up a Jack-n-Coke, and another, and another. She has even taken the doctor's pills, which provided sleep, but no rest. This evening is different. Tonight, the gift chooses her. Into a natal solitude it takes her, the ideal shelter from that which for so long has robbed her sleep.

The fog is in fact so deep that when the doorbell rings, it goes nearly unnoticed. It is just a faint echo. The second ring brings the dull awareness that something outside this womb is calling. She reaches over to nudge Joe and remembers that he isn't there. The idea jolts her. Some, but not all of the fog clears.

"He still has a key." Jen mutters. She pushes back the sheets, fumbles around, finds the lamp switch. She hopes it's him.

It's not.

Just beyond the threshold stand two men. Both are wearing dark blue, one chubby, the other tall. The tall one she thinks she recognizes. "Jennifer Johnson?" He asks. "Your husband is Joseph E. Johnson, right?" Jen nods. They introduce themselves. She doesn't hear their names. They produce their badges. She looks, but doesn't see.

They show Jen a fax. It is a copy of Joe's scuba diver certification card. "Is this your husband?"

Jen glances at the paper. "Yes, of course it is...How did you get this? What's going on?"

"This evening we were contacted by the authorities in Mexico. They sent us this fax."

"Mexico?"

"Your husband is missing and is presumed dead..."

Jen stares vacantly. It is as if they've not spoken. She waits, wondering when they will say something.

"Mrs. Johnson? Would you like to sit down?"

She does not move. "Wh...What was that!?"

"Your husband is missing, ma'am."

They tell the story. "Apparently Mr. Johnson flew to Cozumel this morning."

"Cozumel?"

"He checked into his hotel and then booked a charter to go diving. The dive master said that he'd not met Mr. Johnson before, but he had this card with him. The dive master has confirmed that the picture on the card matched the man who is missing."

"...Cozumel?"

"At some point, Mr. Johnson evidently became disoriented and swam past safe limits. His dive partner saw what was happening. She tried to stop him, but could not. He just swam, deeper and deeper until he was out of sight. The dive master believes the disorientation was due to something called..," the officer unfolds a slip of paper and glances down, "nitrogen narcosis. The boat captain called the Mexican Coast Guard. Together they initiated a search which at sunset was suspended. While coast guard promised that they'd look for him again tomorrow, the place where he went missing is quite deep. They may never find him."

Jen hears nothing. She watches the officer's lips. They move, but there is no sound. Over her eyebrow, she runs three fingers. She feels nothing. Somewhere beneath her lungs, a single syllable rises and repeats itself, a whisper at first and the only thing Jen really hears. As it rises, it fills her lungs with the kind of urgency that comes as one's breath can no longer be held.

"no. no. No. No! NO! NNOOOH!"

She runs to the bedroom and finds her phone. She calls. He does not answer. She calls again. Again. Again. She hears his recorded greeting and shouts over the voice mail instructions. "Come home Joe! Damn you, come home! Come! Home!..." She backs away, two or three half steps. Into a leather easy chair she falls, melts. As she does, that syllable, now mixed with muted sobs, recedes, returning to the place from where it first rose. "NO. No. no..."

"I'm so sorry Mrs. Johnson," the officer pauses, "We need to ask you a few questions. What can you tell us about your husband's trip?"

There is a long silence as she reads his lips and tries to form the words that were never meant to be spoken. "I...I didn't...didn't know he was going...anywhere. You see h...he left. About a week ago. He...he left me. We uh, we agreed to..." Jen hears her own voice trail away. Again she melts. Around her the leather folds. This time there is no return. Her mouth moves. There is no sound.

The tall one asks another question, but by now Jen cannot see his lips. The room with all its sound and silence, all its light and darkness explodes. The walls and ceiling peel themselves away exposing a black and expansive night. It is a blackness brimming with remorse and an expansiveness that cannot contain her guilt. Like the tip of a fountain pen pressed into a paper towel, it saturates the night and spreads its inky hues. Jen's hands, her hair, the chair, the officers, and the threshold, and the squad parked in the driveway, and the cloud covered dome above her, everything large, everything small is stained. Toward her, away from her it seeps until every corner, every edge, every crack fills, and beneath it all the single syllable whispers its futility.

"no. no. no..."

*We live in a 60 mile deep ocean. This ocean is known as the atmosphere and it is filled with a fluid called air. That's right, fluid. While we don't often think in these terms, the water that fills the world's oceans and the air that makes our atmosphere have many similar properties. Both can be weighed and measured. Both exert pressure on the people who inhabit these environments. This exerted pressure is measured in pounds per square inch, or **p.s.i.***

*If we could set on a scale a column of air 1" long by 1" wide by 60 miles high, we would find that it weighs 14.7 lbs. This downward force (or the p.s.i.) is known as 1 atmosphere of pressure (**1 ATM**) and it is a constant. While our bodies are always subject to this pressure, we don't normally notice how air squeezes us. This is because our bodies always exist under these constant circumstances. Thus 14.7 p.s.i. is our native pressure.*

When entering the water, the fluid in which a diver finds himself is more dense and much heavier. The same 14.7 p.s.i. of sea level pressure is achieved in only 33 ft. of water. This means that if a diver descends to 33 ft, he is experiencing 2 ATMs (1 ATM of air pressure and 1 of water). At 66 ft, there are 3 ATMs. At 99 ft, there are 4 ATMs, etc. Put simply, the further beneath the surface a diver descends, the greater the pressure.

Open Water SCUBA Certification Manual
Compiled by DII (Dive Instructors International)
Pg. 41

Chapter 2

(A year and a half before the accident)

THEY SINK INTO THEIR OVERSTUFFED cushions and watch as a couple of carts roll up to the green, and stop. All that stands between the two of them is an end table and a half empty bottle of Malbec. The sun dips low, hanging mid way between the deck awning and the tee box. On the corners of the horizon, hints of orange are etched. In that moment, the world looks permanent, unchangeable, like the watercolor that hangs in Tom's study. Afternoon's gusty wind stills; becomes the nearly imperceptible breath that hints of evening and its cool promise. The carts leave the green and move toward the next tee box. Up the fairway, another scoots. There is nothing to do, but sip wine and watch the sun disappear. This is Annie's favorite part of the day.

It had been a little less than two years since they had finished the house. Tom didn't play golf and still does not, but he knew how much Annie wanted to build and how much she wanted a place here, on the course. Annie called it "her dream", a product of the many years when they'd always struggled, always job jumped, always just made ends meet. So when Pete, Tom's brother, offered Tom the comptroller position at the bank, it was "game on". By week's end, Annie had the lot picked and a meeting with the contractor set. "Those lean days are over," Annie declared, as the backhoe teetered over the curb and pulled up to the string outline that would become their basement.

Eight months and God only knows how many thousands of dollars produced the 3,600 square feet of what Annie now calls perfection. The kitchen, done in cherry and white ice granite, opens to a great room complete with a 20 foot tall cathedral ceiling. On one side, a black tile fireplace lights the hardwood floor. On the other, a glass wall rises the full 20 feet and frames the 13th green. Four bedrooms, three and a half baths, a study, wet bar, exercise center, and a play room for Sophie; it is all stamped with Annie's eye, her love of art deco's clean lines, her attention to detail. Dori, the interior designer calls it her signature project and regularly brings potential clients through. The house does just what it is supposed to do. It makes Annie proud.

Between his fingers, Tom rolls the stem, his glass still half full. He glances behind the bottle and catches Annie's eye. She turns her head slightly laying it against the back of the chair. She says nothing, but offers that slight smile that is only hers. It takes him back, seeing Annie as he first saw her. He was studying Accounting II at Dino's, the campus coffee shop, when she and two of her friends walked through the door. Her long, thick hair swung to one side, and she flashed that same slight smile. Time stopped. Everything stopped. He couldn't move. He couldn't breathe. Was that meant for him? He didn't know, but from that moment, from that breathless, time stopping moment he was certain that this would be the girl that he'd marry. Thirteen years later nothing's the same and everything's the same. Annie was stunning then and still is. She was perfect then and that perfection has aged like the wine rolling over the bottom of his glass. She is the perfect host, the perfect conversationalist, the perfect everything. She is also controlled, difficult, demanding. Most of all, Annie still holds this power. She swings her hair or turns that smile and still she takes his breath away. Still she stops time and he wouldn't have it any other way.

He returns the smile and feels her contentment. It rolls over the end table, around the now empty bottle, and pours into him, warming him in ways he still cannot understand. Building the house was a pain in the ass. Paying for it is an even bigger pain, but Tom doesn't care. Annie's happy and it makes him happy. This is how their life together works and Tom could not be more pleased.

Annie lifts her head just a bit. "Did I tell you that Meg is finally getting her kitchen? Dori brought her by yesterday. This is the *third* time. Meg so loved what we did with everything that she went home and talked to Jeff. They're starting next week."

"Jeeze!" Tom replies, "What did she promise him? Jeff is *such* a tight wad."

"Don't know," Annie giggles, "but whatever it was he caved. She's pretty excited."

Conversation is almost always filled with nothing. That's Annie's way. If it's not some tid-bit from her coffee shop girls or the latest book her club is reading, it's a Des Moines shopping trip, another blouse she brought home, or the new something that will be "perfect on the bedroom wall". Conversation. It's breezy, and it's fun, and it fills the air with one small thing after the next. After all, the way to keep a perfect world perfect is to do just that; fill the air and keep those things small. Of course Tom knows that this is how it works, but it doesn't bother him. It is, in fact, part of his wife's mystique. Her infectiously easy way can redirect any conversation, moving it away from those awkward, delicate, or even explosively stormy seas and into that safe harbor called "Annie's small things". In this respect, Annie is a master navigator; she performs the task so covertly and so seamlessly that no one realizes that it happens. How does she do it? This is, to Tom, a mystery. Most everything about her is a mystery. Her poise, her exterior calm is always in place. There is nothing that causes panic, or at least nothing that anyone can see. In fact, the world around her could be crumbling and her illusion of confidence would remain effortless and so completely natural that there's not a soul alive who wouldn't believe everything is under control.

Tom loves this about his wife and wishes that he could be the same way.

The sun is now completely gone. Around the perimeter of the house, the lawn lighting pops on, its glow painting delicate accents. Evening is cool, but otherwise this has become such a perfect night that Annie wants another bottle. Tom unfolds a blanket, covers her feet, and heads for the wine rack. As he does, he walks by the study, where he catches a glimpse of his antique roll top. This desk does not fit Annie's modern decor, but because it was Tom's grandfather's Annie wanted him to keep it. She simply decorated around the desk, filling his study with new things that look old. The desk returns the glimpse and does so in a way that chills him. The top is rolled shut and locked. Tom doesn't know why exactly he locks it. He just does. He sees underneath, where it is so dark that nothing can be seen. He feels around and finds the stacks of envelopes he knows are there, 3 of them each 2 inches tall. The envelopes are neatly kept, all facing the same direction. All have thin slits cut across the tops. They contain secret information, names and numbers known only to Tom. They speak only to Tom. One by one, each envelop states its claim. The roll call sounds mechanical, like the automated female voice Tom hears when he calls the 800 numbers that are printed on the back of his credit cards. *Club Dues: $637. First Bank Visa: $16,384.24. Central Bank Visa: $18,879.15. The Lexus: $406. Discover: $12,321.13. Gas and Electric: $277. The Navigator: $391. The mortgage: $2,760. Another Visa: $9,348.57. Cable: $68.19 Garbage and sewer: $94.37.*

    Another.

        Another.

            Another...

Each takes its turn. When the final envelope speaks, they start over, one after the next. Again. Again. Again. He alone hears them. He alone carries their weight. He alone feels the due dates squeeze him. He so wishes he could be more like Annie, but he also knows that these are voices Annie would never want to hear.

    They follow him,

        the wine rack, *Club dues: 637,*

            the kitchen, *1st Bank: 16,384,*

                and the deck, where Tom resumes his position, fills the glasses, and sets the half empty bottle between them. In turn, the envelopes speak.

        Central Visa.

        The Lexus.

        Discover.

Annie picks up the conversation right where she left off. "When do Joe and Jen get back?"

The voices drop to a whisper. It is as if they are aware that Annie might be listening.

"Tomorrow."

"I can't believe she actually went diving!" Annie continues, almost as though she hasn't heard Tom's reply, "Jen's always been a beach kind of girl. You know...park her buns on the chaise, worship the sun, and have Pedro bring the drinks. That's what the two of us do...that and wait for you two to get off your dive boat."

Gas and Electric: 277

"Poor baby." Tom reaches over and mockingly strokes her hand. "It's a tough life, isn't it?"

The Navigator: 391

Annie giggles. "Well, I hope she is havin' fun."

The Mortgage: 2760

Cozumel. It was five years ago when Annie and Jen first floated the idea. A Caribbean vacation didn't take much convincing. The winter blues were hitting Tom hard and Joe's contracting business was driving him crazy, so Jen found the flight and Annie booked *Laguna Azul,* a hotel right beside the international pier. The week was pure magic. For Jen and Annie, it was the seaside morning coffees, strolling the plaza square, sun dress dickering, candlelight suppers, relaxing beneath a palapa and watching the sun set. For Joe and Tom, it was diving. Of course they'd planned only to snorkel, but some guy the dive shop paid to hawk the beach stood over their hammocks and signed them up. That afternoon they took the resort course, a one day scuba introduction. The next morning they were boat diving. From the moment they sank beneath the surface and breathed their first underwater air, they were hooked. They had entered a world of complete freedom, a world where physics' normal rules did not apply and all the vise grip pressures that kept the two of them tightly wound completely disappeared. Before the boat left the reef, Tom and Joe made a pact. They'd get certified. They'd be back.

That first adventure produced a series of others, all of them back to *Laguna Azul*. There had been four-some trips; last minute trips, girl trips, and guy trips, but this was the first time Joe and Jen traveled by themselves.

The wine begins to do its work and into his glass Tom happily descends. He pictures the reef, and listens as Annie spins her tales. It is nothing he hasn't heard before, but like one of Joe's bonfires, her soft excitement lights the darkness and he finds himself drifting. To a faraway place, it carries him, where immersed in crystal waters and surrounded by bright corals, he is free. Annie, her gentle glow, her hypnotic spell transfixes him.

Time stops, and for a moment he thinks that the voices have as well.

Chapter 3

THERE IS A CLOUD COVER, not a good star gazing night, but Joe doesn't know where else he might go. He doesn't want to bump into Jeff Kingly or any of the other regulars, so he avoids Sparky's, the local pub. He won't walk into the house. Right now, he can't even see Tom, so he piles wood, loads the pit, more than usual, and feels it burn. The dry logs crack, shooting orange tracers that scatter randomly and disappear. Above his head, flames twist, throwing strobe-like flashes that dissect his movements and create a series of stop action snap shots. A wall of heat slaps Joe's thighs and face. The intensity forces him a half step backward. At the same time, chills climb around his shoulders and over his calves, everything facing the night. He lifts his beer, sets it against his lips, flips the bottom up, and with the back of his thumb wipes clean his chin. "Fire and life," he thinks to himself, "nothing's ever quite the way it should be."

Joe glances toward the house and sees Jen. In and out of the kitchen window she moves. In their own light each of them is bathed. For Jen it's the florescent tubes and their cool blue and for Joe it's his orange bonfire and its stark lines and deep shadows. Between the two of them lies a dark abyss. Into a night with no other light, the back yard trees, the shed, Jen's empty flower garden, and the path that connects house and pit have all disappeared. The entire world consists of Jen's window and Joe's fire. In this otherwise black eternity, these two tiny islands are lost, without so much as a single star to navigate the gulf between them.

He wants to go in the house, talk with her, but doesn't know how to get there.

Joe picks up a piece of firewood, a wedge split from a locust trunk, and studies it. Along the grain he runs his fingers, following thin lines that narrow, sweep sideways, widen, and finally curve in behind a knot. It looks like a river current, fast water sweeping around a partially submerged boulder. Joe eyes the piece and smiles. Imperfections making this plain thing unique, weaknesses becoming the creative force that pushes and pulls the wood until it is transformed, until it becomes a graceful, sweeping beauty; it fascinates him. It inspires awe. The contradiction also raises his curiosity. "How it is that defects and blemishes make the piece so interesting, so pleasing to the eye, so...right?" He also wonders why this is so unlike the rest of his life. Maybe this is why he became a carpenter; to wonder, to figure such things out.

As Joe flips the wedge into the pit, he notices a flashlight beam bouncing toward him. He hopes it's her.

It's not.

"Hey Puck!" Joe recognizes Tom's smiling voice. "What's up? Thought you'd have called me by now."

Puck, it's a name that came from some pretty carefree days, when, as Jen puts it, "the IQ was low, testosterone levels were off the charts, and the only worry was how the two of them would stay ahead of Tom's old man." Joe, on the other hand, could talk his folks into most anything, so one winter, the two of them cooked up a particularly inventive plan. They'd build a hockey rink. Joe got the ok. His father moved the cars, and the boys prepared the Johnson driveway, scraping it down to the concrete. Evenly around the edges, they piled the snow. Next they cut up an old blue bed sheet, made four inch strips, and laid down a center line. Up from the basement window they ran a hose, turned on the water, and applied eight coats. When it was done, the driveway was a thing of beauty, it looked like polished glass.

The fun lasted about two weeks and came to an end when Joe put a slapshot through his bedroom window. After that, Mr. Johnson took the hockey sticks, salted down the driveway, and Joe became "Puck". The name stuck.

This and a hundred other stunts they pulled sealed a friendship that endured those usually irresistible currents that so often send people drifting apart. As for everyone else, grade school playmates have dropped off the face of the planet, high school buddies have become the kind of casual acquaintances that get renewed at the every five year reunions, but Tom and Puck have never missed a beat. The hours they spent shooting hoops and hanging from the jungle gym set a foundation deeper than graduation, deeper than moves, deeper than girlfriends, deeper than everything that pulls even the best of friends apart. Of course, the two of them have developed other interests, like bonfires, and star gazing, and diving, but the foundation remains as solid as the day it was first poured. These are just the newest countries through which their friendship travels.

"Hey Hyden." Joe nods toward the woodpile where in the niches, five bottles are cradled, "Grab a brew."

Tom wraps his fingers around a brown neck and twists the cap which he tosses into the fire. "So how was it?"

"Palencar Gardens was amazing as ever." Joe replied, "Did a night dive around the cruise ships, and at Columbia Shallows we splashed in on three spotted eagle rays.[1]"

"Really! What did Jen think?"

Joe pauses. The change in his tone is nearly imperceptible. "She liked it."

"Whaddya mean 'she liked it'? Something happen, Puck?"

"Well, let's just say that this was not the vacation we intended." Joe pauses, measures his words. "Fact is we took off together to try to work things out. You know, kind of jumpstart things. Plan backfired. Go figure."

"I didn't know..." Actually Tom does know. For over a year, he's known. Until this minute, it remained an unspoken matter, no whats, or whys, or hows. Tom has just known that something is amiss. He feels it every time he sees Joe and Jen together and marks the change in the way they treat each other. He senses it when Joe is drinking his beer or feeding the pit. In his friend and even between the two of them (Puck and Tom) there is a marked distance. A couple of times Tom has tried to pry information, but Puck's curt deflections were a cue to "leave it alone", so he did.

"When did this start, Puck?"

"It's been bubbling for a long time, Hyden. A long, long time." There is a silence. "Kind of hard to talk about."

"Nuts," Tom whispers.

"Yeah..."

---

1. A type of ray, dark blue or black with white spots. Adult Spotted Eagle Rays will have a wing span of up to 10 feet.

Tom wants to ask more, get a few details, but he thinks better. Knowing what not to say and when not to say it, this is why their friendship has lasted. The two of them sip beer and watch wood dissolve. For a long time they stand there. Nothing else is spoken and it is a good nothing. The fire needs feeding, but neither of them moves. Darkness creeps toward the center of the pit. The night offers its usual silence. They listen, each of them searching for a comfort that they know it can't possibly contain. Finally, Tom turns toward the path and as he walks away lays a hand over Joe's shoulder. "You know where I am, Puck."

Alone again, Joe glances toward the house. He waits. He sees the kitchen window go dark and then watches. On and off the lights are switched; the hallway, the bathroom, and finally their bedroom. One last time the fire flickers. He throws back the bottom of the bottle, finds the path, feels his way toward the house.

Chapter 4

Cupboard. Glass.
    Cupboard to the fridge. Ice.
        Fridge to the cabinet. Coke. Jack. Equal parts.
    Cabinet to the sink.

THE TELEVISION BESIDE THE MICROWAVE glows. Colors change. Jen lowers the volume until the sound becomes nearly nothing. The news anchor whispers. She brings an update on last week's top story, the people of Mongolia and ground water arsenic levels. While no one knows how it got there, the unabated arsenic could become deadly. Tests indicate a concentration of .07 parts per million, an amount that, over time, will poison anyone who drinks from these wells. "To gain some perspective," the anchor reports, ".07 parts per million is equivalent to a cup of arsenic in an Olympic sized swimming pool..."

Jen takes a sip, kills the tube, and strains, looking through the window and its glare. At first, all she sees is her own reflection if it can be called that. It is in fact little more than a shadow. The light above the sink creates an effect that at once illuminates and mutes her curls, her narrow nose, her thin lips. The image looks ghostly and unfamiliar, as if it is there and it is not there. It is more like a hole in the glass than a reflection. Jen strains more and moves the hole until it frames and centers a couple of objects, an orange blaze and Joe, his outline silhouetted against the flame. The two things seem to be one. It is as if without the outline there is no fire and without the fire there is no outline. In the hole, the two things float, hanging directly between the place where her eyes have nearly disappeared.

Jen cannot remember a time she didn't know him. Same street, same school, same church, Joe was always somewhere near, always a part of her known world. Of course at first, he was just there, just one of eight neighborhood boys. About the only thing that made Joe remarkable was Tom, and that just because one was never seen without the other. Not only were the two always together, but they acted as a magnetic force that gathered the others. Around them a guy's club formed, an outfit that had a single regulation, no girls. The rule was strictly enforced until the day they were short an outfielder. Jen, who by virtue of her gender was always consigned to the edges, would have to do. It was a rare opportunity and Jen knew that if she was going to prove herself, the time was now. She made the most of the moment by jacking an unhittable pitch and sending it so far over their heads that she walked the bases.

From that moment on, the guys took her seriously, everyone that is, except Joe who teased the hell out of her. Years later, he confessed that this was the moment he fell in love. Of course at the time, all Jen knew was that finally she'd earned the respect she deserved and she wasn't going to let some jerk screw things up. He teased her. She fought back. First, it was Jen then Joe, Joe then Jen, one insult after the next, one jab after another. She never called him Puck. She knew he liked the name and this was her way of pissing him off. Instead and out of nowhere, she would appear and call to him. "O lover boy!" Then she would turn on her heels and holler "Kiss my, butt!" This of course made him chase her all the more, made him tease her all the more, and made her dislike him all the more. The banter escalated, became rancor, then it morphed into a real warfare fired by a real and passionate hatred. Around the neighborhood, their mutual disdain was the stuff of legend, lasting through grade school, junior high, and into high school.

It was fall of their senior year, a Friday night home game. Jen, who was a marching band trombonist, was among the last to leave the stadium. She walked across a nearly empty parking lot and noticed that someone was sitting on the hood of her car.

"I love a woman in uniform." She recognizes the voice.

"Get lost Johnson."

Off the hood, Joe slides. "Why don't we stop pretending?"

Instinct takes over. Like a hunted rabbit she freezes. "What the hell are you talking about?"

"Com' on Jen. You know."

Jen reaches for the door, but Joe leans against it, his hip covering the handle. Now they are close, nearly touching. He extends an index finger. Over her eyebrow and down the side of her cheek, he gently draws a line. Just as gently and to her complete surprise Jen leans, her cheek falling into the line so that first his finger then his palm becomes a cradle on which she rests her head. In an instant, she feels the laws of gravity shift. Like so much loose gravel rolling underneath her feet, all those years of violent disdain flip and become an irresistible desire. Beneath her breath she whispers, "What the hell is going on?"

"You know, Jen. You know."

If their hatred was stormy, their love affair was a freak of nature, a category five hurricane with no eye and no calm. Once intentions were openly declared, passion was completely unbridled. With a new and more intense contempt, they fought only with an equally intense desire, to fall into each other's arms.

One way then the other.

    Back and forth.

        Breakup. Makeup.

            War. Romance.

                Rage. Desire.

Hatred fueled love and love fueled hatred. Every swing of the pendulum was as violently, wildly intense as the other. This was the oxygen rich blood that coursed through the veins of their life together. Passion, "balls to the wall" passion, it was the thing that defined them both. Tom always said that "be it love or be it war...either way they'd go, it'd take a crowbar to pull them apart", and he was spot-on correct.

They graduated in May and married in July. Tom's wedding gift was over the top, a grandfather clock and a crow bar. To this day, the two pieces grace the Johnson living room, displayed together as though they are some liturgical appointment.

That fall Joe enrolled in trade school and Jen became a grocery store checker. Back and forth the pendulum swung. Life was good.

    She looks in her glass.

        It is empty.

    She goes to the fridge,

        from the fridge to the cabinet,

            from the cabinet to the window.

"It was just a baby." She mouths words that almost make a sound, "Such a small thing."

From the day they got married, Jen was ready to start a family. Joe insisted that they wait. He wanted to get school behind them. He first wanted a good job, maybe even build a nest egg so that he could properly support their children. They fought. They made up. The pendulum swung. Finally Joe relented.

Becoming pregnant took years.

Years.

Years of lovemaking and heartbreak.

Lovemaking and heartbreak.

Doctor appointments and hope.

Hope and lovemaking.

Lovemaking and heartbreak.

The doctor sat them down, told them that they'd exhausted the possibilities and should now consider other options. This of course made Jen all the more determined. They kept trying and when finally it happened, no one could believe it. The ultrasound confirmed what Jen already knew. The doctor called him a miracle. Cradled in her womb, the baby grew and she loved him. More than life itself, Jen loved him. They gave him a name, Joe Jr, *Joey*. They spent their evenings sprawled on the living room floor, the television on, but unwatched. Jen propped herself against the couch and Joe laid perpendicular to her, his arm around her belly and his ear resting gently atop the mound. He'd listen. Together they'd sing soft lullabies and feel Joey kick. For the first time in her life, Jen, the queen of restless intensity, was settled.

It was during delivery. Something happened. What? Who the hell knows. The heart monitor first buzzed then flat-lined. The doctor barked orders. In and out of nowhere nurses rushed around the room, brought this, carried that. When it was over, they called it oxygen deprivation, swallowing meconium, something like that.

Gloved hands laid Joey into Jen's arms. The doctor told her it wouldn't be long. Jen held him. With all her life she held him. She studied his tiny hands and perfect face. She rocked him and sung the lullabies he already knew. Tightly. Tightly she held him...until he drifted away.

After that Jen just didn't care. Nothing mattered, not work, not home, not Joe. Fighting and passion fused, first becoming a numbed fog, then a strange lethargy, then a comfortable routine. When the fighting did resume, it was dislodged, disconnected. The pendulum was broken and dysfunctional, their fighting twisted. The arguments took on a life all their own, a life predicated on the kind of dull self-centeredness that breeds anything, but love.

This was their cup of acid, odorless, tasteless, colorless acid silently polluting their well of life. Over the next couple of years it poisoned her, poisoned him, poisoned them. In waters tainted by indifference, their fiery relationship slowly extinguished. She had become an empty shell and there wasn't a damned thing she could do about it.

Above the sink, a light glares.
    Into the window, Jen stares.
        Everything is a shadow,
            faint, ghostly reflections,
                holes,
        like the one through which she now sees him.
Into her glass, she looks.
    It is empty.
She goes to the fridge,
    from the fridge to the cabinet,
        from the cabinet to the window.
The fire is gone and with it the outline,
    or is the outline gone and with it the fire?

~ David Grindberg ~

    She doesn't know.
She wants to cry.
    She can't...

Chapter 5

Tom throws his hip against the service door. The door violently swings, hits a rubber stop, thuds, and rebounds, just missing his shoulder. Across the lot, he briskly cuts a diagonal, fumbles around, finds his keys.

Pete's completely unnecessary meeting ran long and delays Tom's day-end responsibilities. It is now late afternoon, not what he plans, but it is what he has come to expect. What's worse is that Pete knew better. Tom was in a hurry and Pete purposely wasted his time, prattling on about Calvin Jenkins, president of Pulaski Federal Bank, and "all the 'overtime' Cal and his administrative assistant are logging." By the time Tom is dismissed he's ready to blow a gasket. "The world could be coming to an end," he plops behind the wheel and slams shut the car door, "but when little brother says jump…"

Five years ago Tom's younger brother, Peter Franklin Hyden, was named president of Lakeland Savings and Trust, taking the helm from their father, Franklin Thomas Hyden (Frank). Years before, Frank had stepped into his father's shoes, who had, in turn, stepped into his father's shoes. For nearly every one of Lake Pulaski's 14,000 residents, Pete's appointment was a complete surprise. Convention stipulated that the oldest Hyden son would inherit this position, but somewhere along the line, the old man decided that "Tom didn't have the chops for the job."

Four generations, eighty-seven years cultivating and refining a "trademark of respectability", has made the Hyden name Lake Pulaski's premier brand. Pete, of course, happily plays his scripted part. He is articulate, savvy, and has perfected Frank's benevolent swagger. He also understands the value of the Hyden currency and zealously protects it. Thus when Pete made Tom the bank's vice president and comptroller, it was a move that not only "saved Tom" from his *Davis and Sons* dead-end position, but also came with two caveats, a warning to "not screw up" and a reminder of the responsibility that accompanies his last name.

Pete sounds so much like the old man, that once in a while he turns Tom into the six year old who could never meet his father's expectations. Most of the time, though, the thought of Pete just makes Tom want to puke.

Tom points the Lexus toward Main Street and in his rear view mirror sees the bank diminish. Watching monuments to the self-important shrink, particularly this one, gives him an odd satisfaction, and he wishes that his little corner of the world contained more of these mirrors.

In truth, he likes his job. He understands the numbers and they understand him. He loves his spreadsheets, filling his rows, arranging his columns, watching everything balance. *Account name. Loan Amount. Amount Due. Amount Paid. Remaining Balance.* Across the rows he runs his fingers knowing that each one represents another business, another client, another life that, on a single line, can be summarized. One row is white, the next gray, weaving an alternating pattern that looks like one of Annie's modern tapestries. To Tom, these interlaced numbers are a thing of beauty, and if at day's end the tapestry is not perfect, if something of this beauty is missing and things don't add up, it's just a mystery that must be solved. Usually the answer is right before his eyes, a couple of digits transposed, an extra zero playing hide and seek. Tom plays along. He finds the error and watches the totals recalculate their approval. Of course, this is as close to game playing as ledgers ever come. They are by their very nature logical, simple, and most of all genuine. They are not full of themselves. They do not pretend to be important or need to be noticed. There's no guessing what they might be thinking or listening as they cut down people who are not around and thus cannot defend themselves. They are just numbers. Only in his ledgers do they exist. This is their place in the world and here they are comfortable. They add up. They balance. They are in every sense of the word predictable, and Tom finds that working with them is deeply satisfying. Yes, he likes his job. It's the people or rather the person he can't stand. It's the portraits, all four generations of them. They hang in the bank lobby and look down upon the one Hyden who they have decided doesn't "add up". This is what he hates.

It takes a few minutes, but Tom finally cools down and remembers the assignment Annie gave him. He quickly calculates an ETA and decides that even without the pit stop he'll be lucky to make the recital. "Sophie will have to live without the bouquet," he thinks aloud.

Normally, the drive from one end of town to the other takes 15 minutes, but today Tom can see that the lights will work against him. He cuts a corner, angles down a side street, avoids all the stop-and-goes. He knows exactly where to turn and where not to turn. He sees everything, Lake Pulaski's grid of parkways, avenues and alleys, low traffic neighborhoods, busy intersections, routes that could possibly shave minutes. The ease with which the Lexus stitches this pattern is directly related to the way Tom has been stitched, how he and the ground beneath the grid are bonded. This is more than mere familiarity. It is knowing…knowing people, and habits, and time of day. It is understanding that everything and everyone, himself included, are pieces of a whole. There are no individuals here, just threads woven together. They form a single blanket which, in turn, is sewn into Iowa's rich, black dirt and the cycles it inspires; spring and fall, planting and harvest, life and death. On this primal level, all the threads shrink, shed their egos, and mesh into the pattern of things. Tom's mastery of the grid, Pete's bloviating, Frank's stingy approval, the garden variety pretense and phoniness that constitutes the way people treat each other, the town, the generations and the way they come and go, everything is humbled. Within this immense rolling blanket and its poetic rhythms, all things are seen for what they really are.

~~~~~~~~~~~~~~

Sophie is almost eight. She has Annie's looks, her thick hair, and that contagious smile. She did not inherit her mother's shape. To remedy this, Annie has developed a *nutrition plan*, ensuring that meals are healthy, portions are limited, and the refrigerator is stocked with apple slices and yogurt.

Tom is not so worried. "It's just a little left over baby fat." He tells his wife. "It's cute and she'll soon grow out of it. Just let the poor kid be a kid."

Knowing that these protests fall upon deaf ears, Tom takes it upon himself to occasionally slip Sophie some contraband. When Annie takes off for book club or plans a Des Moines shopping excursion, the two of them have "date night". This is their secret code for a trip to the Burger Barn where Sophie orders her favorite meal, a double cheese, fries, and a chocolate shake. While they eat, Tom fits himself with the Burger Barn cardboard cow horns. He snorts and paws the ground until he makes Sophie laugh. Next, he pulls out crayons and together they color the place mat pictures or play tic tac toe. By the time they walk across the parking lot, the two of them are hand in hand, giggling about the date, and in agreement that "it would be best if mommy didn't know." Daddy is as smitten with his little girl as he is the woman who brought Sophie into the world.

Tom slips through the back door and locates Annie who has saved him a spot. Today is Sophie's gymnastics recital and graduation day. It was three years ago when Annie, "knowing how much Sophie wanted to perfect the balance beam," called Northern Iowa Gymnastics Center and enrolled her. Sophie spent the first couple of years learning posture, then tumbling, then basic floor exercises. Now she is working a beam that sits just a few inches above the floor. A successful recital will take her to the next step, the beam at regulation height. This is a big day.

Tom squeezes over four pair of knees and sits next to his wife.

"Forget the flowers?" Annie whispers.

"Pete." Tom replies.

This is all he needs to say. Annie smiles and knowingly nods. She shares Tom's resentment. Ever since Pete "saved Tom's bacon," both he and Kelly, Pete's wife, have been completely insufferable. "They act so smug," Annie vigorously complains, "like you should remain in perpetual pucker." The whole business drives her crazy.

He scans the line of gymnasts and immediately finds his little girl. Scarlet spandex stretches over Sophie's form, revealing soft, round lines that gracefully charm her movements. A field of silver sequins creates a sash across her tummy, giving it the appearance of a small, sparkling pot. It is the kind of chubby that has Sophie looking two years younger than she really is and Tom thinks she is perfect. He catches her eye, smiles, winks. Of course Sophie, who is supposed to be concentrating, can't help herself. She turns her head just enough so that Tom can see her entire face, winks with both eyes, then refocuses.

Annie raises her video camera and pushes the record, button. Tom is glad that she has assumed this responsibility. Following Sophie through a four inch screen will not do, not today. He wants to be here, in this moment, with nothing between them. He wants to absorb every subtle movement, his eyes gently embracing the scarlet spandex, the sparkling pot, and especially the girl inside. The music begins and over the beam her round lines sweep. Sophie bites her lower lip and sets her brow. It is Annie's determined concentration in miniature and it is beautiful. She is beautiful.

Then somewhere toward the end of the performance, Sophie begins losing her balance. Her arms roll above her and make small circles. At the waist she bends, her upper body counterbalancing an unseen force. For a moment it looks as if everything is working against her. Tom feels himself bending with her; an effort that evidently pays off. The circles stop, her arms, still off center, freeze, and she brings her torso upright. Once she reclaims her balance, Sophie completes two more elements and her dismount, a hop off the end of the beam. Into the mat she solidly plants both feet, arches her back, and extends her hands upward, forming a V above her head. The audience politely claps. She scans the crowd, spots a beaming Annie. Sophie beams with her.

The program ends and Sophie runs into her mother's arms. She knows that today she makes Annie proud and is ready to bask in the approval. Today Annie does not disappoint.

"Oh Sophie," Annie wraps the words around her, "You were wonderful!"

"Hey princess," Tom chimes in, "way to go."

Tom watches Annie admire Sophie, who like a thirsty puppy laps up the praise. These moments warm him, almost bring him to tears. When it comes to the two of them, this is what he always wants, yet it seldom happens and that seldomness bears a weight upon his heart, a weight that never completely vanishes. This is not to say that Annie's parenting doesn't meet his approval. In so many ways, Annie is so good to Sophie, so attentive, so caring. Yet he also knows that when Annie looks at their daughter, what she sees is a "vast and wonderful potential." She sees a child who needs a mother's strength, a mother's guidance. Annie believes that Sophie needs someone who will foster her development, encourage her potential, and when necessary push her so that eventually she will become the woman Annie knows she can be.

When Tom looks at Sophie, what he sees is a little girl with a tender heart, a heart aching for love.

Chapter 6

Tom's day begins early. It nearly always does. Not that he wants it this way. No, he would prefer a full night's rest. For most people, hot coffee's aroma or the kitchen television's muted sounds gently rouse them, but with Tom that almost never happens. There are instead a hundred things that take their turn and he's never sure which will be next. Annie, Sophie, Puck and Jen, Pete, a plugged drain, a water softener needing his attention, good things, bad things, past, future; they nudge him, gently to be sure, but none the less they nudge him. Quietly they tap his shoulder and from sleep's shallows they lift him. He looks. He listens. He lies there, silently, motionless, so as not to disturb his Annie.

Of course every night is a little different. Sometimes these sessions run like an amateur highlight reel, like the yellowing clips of his father's super 8 movies have been spliced together. Sometimes it is a single photo that sits in memory's wallet; Sophie riding her bike, Annie curled up on the couch and reading a novel, or best of all, Pete in mid-sentence frozen, mouth agape and face contorted as though he's some comic book terrorist.

At the ceiling Tom stares, smiles, and again watches Sophie's triumph. The video includes slow motion replays, Sophie's routine and then the warmth she and her mother share. The smile disappears as he next rewinds the tiff. Annie's militant insistence that "little brother needs to be put in his place" is so strident that Tom actually finds himself defending the jerk. Finally, there is the roll top; the damned roll top. Regardless of where these nights begin, they almost always end here, his grandfather's desk, the locked lid, the darkness, the three stacks of neatly kept envelopes. In a chorus of voices, the envelopes whisper their secrets. With accusations of irresponsibility, they fill his nights.

The numbers contained within the envelopes are different than those of the bank. These are not someone else's numbers. There is no spread sheet here, no gray and white weavings that dispassionately confine their threat. No, these are *his* numbers. They represent his life and his utter failure. He cannot remember when they eluded his control or how they became so wild that a ledger could no longer keep them chained. All he knows is that these envelopes, once a mono-toned annoyance, have become a pack of unleashed Rottweilers, mad dogs backing him into a corner. They threaten him and the family he loves and Tom finds that he will do whatever it takes. He will protect Annie and Sophie.

Telling Annie... How many times has he tried? He can tell her anything else, anything, and she is so good. In fact with Annie, the bigger the screw up the more gentle she becomes. When Meyers and Associates issued their pink slip, he came home and without so much as a word she knew. It was as if the fear in Tom's eyes brought out her very best. With an indescribable tenderness and the calming assurance that belongs only to Annie, she lowered her voice and gently touched his deepest fears. She extended herself around him and as she did Tom knew that everything would be okay. What she does for him is magic, pure and simple magic. This is Annie's protective shell and it makes his big things so small. But this? This is different. No matter how many times he tries, he cannot bring himself to tell her. There is, to this, a terrible shame, a deep and dirty darkness that permeates his soul. Failure, there is no other word for it, the kind of which he cannot let anyone see. No, Annie doesn't know a thing about the Rottweilers and never will.

In the end, this mess is his doing, his completely. The house, the cars, the wardrobes, the thousands upon thousands of nothings Annie brought home. He could have said no. He probably should have said no, and while she wouldn't have liked it, she would have understood. Tom *wants* Annie to have all these things. He loves to see her so happy and knows that someday he will fix the mess, but for now, all he can do is find this high ledge and, with bits of red meat, pacify the dogs. For now, he handles each envelope, removing the contents, unfolding the pages, reading the numbers, asking for patience. For now he puts the numbers back in their envelopes, moves them from pile to pile, and adjusts his priorities, deciding what gets paid today, what gets paid next week, what gets paid next month. A few envelopes are shredded. Most take their new place in the reordered piles. This, at least for the moment, calms the beasts, but of course here in the middle of the night, every calm is temporary. Here, where hungry dogs stalk him, nothing really gets fixed and nothing is ever solved. Time inches toward daybreak and does so in ways that have no purposeful conclusion.

Hanging precariously, seeking an illusive balance, this is how Tom begins his days. So much works against him. There is the gravity that pulls Annie and Sophie apart. There is Pete and his knack for undermining Tom's confidence. There are hungry dogs that sit beneath his ledge and show their teeth. Sometimes Tom feels like he is Sophie working the beam, unsteadily waving her arms, bending, twisting, feverishly seeking a grace filled recovery. Except with Tom it seems as if a place or time for dismount never comes. On his shoulders the entire world wobbles and beneath him there is no floor, no landing point, no soft mat. The deep nothing into which he could fall is terrifying.

Throughout the night, Tom checks his phone. 2:56 a.m. 3:14. 3:27. Between ledge and phone he teeters until finally something he calls "the drift" arrives. When it appears, and it doesn't always, it comes as a voice, invitingly hypnotic, almost imperceptible. It sounds something like Annie's voice, but he knows that it is not. He thinks he hears it call him by name, not "Tom" with the air of casual familiarity, but "Thomas" with protection's gently intimate timbre. Over and over again it whispers. The voice is so soft that he's not sure he hears anything, yet somehow it knows him. It knows him perfectly. It even sees where Tom hides his dark and dirty core and it does not find this ugliness repulsive. In all of Tom's world, this is the one place that confers a complete and unqualified approval. With the weight of a thin cotton cloth, it covers him. It brushes lightly over his temple and around his neck, and leads him beneath the surface of the night where halfway between consciousness and slumber Tom hovers. "The drift" is an odd and strangely wonderful state. Those claims that earlier tapped upon his shoulder and brought him above night's first sleep are still there, but are now weightless and distant. Their urgency seeps through the cotton and dissipates someplace far above. It is like drift-diving the Santa Rosa Wall, cool and dreamlike with a steady two knot current that effortlessly carries him wherever it will, and peacefully takes him through the remainder of the night.

Annie has her favorite part of the day. This is his.

Chapter 7

Www...Wwwwh

Wwwwhhhhhhaaeeeeeeeee

ABOVE A TRANSLUCENT BLUE RING, the stainless steel tea kettle breathes. The pot shudders, awakens, singing a shrill anthem and dancing the kind of frantic jig that has the base rattling against the burner. Just inside the pantry, Annie finishes filling the press, freshly ground Kenya AA. She hurries to the cook top and twists the knob. The blue ring diminishes, becomes a delicate lace, the bright song a silent breath. The dance tapers until the kettle is nearly still.

Annie isn't sure, but she thinks Tom has had another restless night and hopes that if he is still in bed, he could stay there, maybe get a bit more sleep. "I don't want to wake the poor guy," she thinks as she pours the bubbling liquid and watches the grounds roll. Annie knows that even the smallest matters eat him alive, and she wishes he could see things differently.

Steam puffs above the press and vanishes, releasing a rich aroma that reaches around the kitchen and down the hallway. Annie lets the coffee steep. The television, which has been on all morning, is tuned to *Women of Power with Dr. Lisa Buckingham*. From beneath the island, Annie pulls a stool and slides onto the padded seat. Under her elbow are a couple of ads and a copy of Dr. Lisa's latest book, *The Me I Deserve to Be: Inner Strength and the Calm it Creates*. She finds the remote and increases the volume, reaches for a note pad, begins her day-planning.

Things to Do!
- ☐ <u>**Fix things w/ Tom.**</u>

    Dr. Lisa says: "Inner strength leads to outer calm."

    Annie underlines this first chore.
- ☐ **Pack Sophie's lunch—pick up Meg's girls–get everyone to School.**

    Dr. Lisa says: "Big meanings are found in small jobs."
- ☐ **Lunch with Dori—discuss adding a new motif to the kitchen.**

    Dr. Lisa says: "Visualize what you want and how you will make it happen."
- ☐ **Open the house for one of Dori's clients—set out refreshments.**

    Dr. Lisa says: "Others will feed off the positive energy you project, lifting them up with you."
- ☐ **Go over recital video w/ Sophie.**

    Dr. Lisa says: "To become The Me I Deserve to Be, you must center yourself on the task at hand."

Annie loves these bits of wisdom and weaves them into her day. Their cadence, their poetic brevity are easily remembered and for her become refrains of guidance.

The opening credits have run. The camera pans the audience then finds Dr. Lisa and her warm smile. Annie pushes aside her note pad and centers herself. Lisa's chestnut hair is up and tightly pulled. With her every movement, the pony tail cheerfully bobs. White slacks accentuate her long legs and a pastel yellow top is as tastefully understated as the makeup she wears. A boom microphone is clipped behind her ear and frees both hands. She walks around the stage and through the audience, doing so in a way that is both relaxed and purposeful. The talks are not flamboyant and not theatrical, just confident, conversational, and most of all genuine. There is, in fact, something so real about Dr. Lisa that Annie believes she could be a good friend, maybe even a sister. The two of them look alike, think alike, and see the world in exactly the same way. Annie often imagines that if she and Lisa were sitting on the deck and sharing a bottle of wine, they could finish each other's sentences.

Today Dr. Lisa's talk is entitled "Lessons from the Hermit Crab."

"When I was a little girl, I used to go to the beach and play with the hermit crabs. You've all seen them–little critters that climb into abandoned sea shells and use them as their homes. A crab will live in her shell until she outgrows it. Then she begins the house hunt. You've all done your fair share of house shopping, right?" As she delivers this line, Dr. Lisa directs the question at a middle aged audience member. Lisa smiles. The woman smiles back. "So Ms. Crab finds the right home, not too big and not too small, and makes the move. For the crab, that shell is more than just a home, it is her armor, her protection. As soon as Ms. Crab senses danger, she pulls back as far into the shell as she can, and she stays there until the threat has passed." Lisa says, "We all need these shells. We all have sensitive parts of our lives that need armor. The key is to do so with grace and style. Let everyone think that you are the shell and the shell is you. Now let's meet our new homeowner." The picture cuts from Dr. Lisa to her PowerPoint and a closeup of a hermit crab. Her delicate legs are holding the shell above the sand. Over the top of the shell, bullet points appear.

1) Size Matters.

Lisa explains, "You need a shell that's the right size. It needs to be large enough so that it will contain all that you are. Remember, be vulnerable only when you want to be vulnerable and with whom you want to be vulnerable. That's why you have the right sized shell, so that when you need the armor, you are fully covered."

2) Keep Your Interests Mobile.

"You need to be able to move from shell to shell. If you grow out of one, don't hesitate. Go out and do a little house hunting. Find another."

3) Functionality AND Beauty.

"You need a shell that is not only functional, that not only protects, but is also beautiful." Lisa points, "Look at the smooth, round lines. Look at the subtle colors. When folks see your shell, they see your strength. They see the way your outer beauty is a projection of that inner strength, and they want to be around you. Most of all, they want to know your secret. They'll look at you and be asking themselves, 'How does she do it?'"

Annie thinks about her own shell and how strong, how self sufficient, and most of all how beautiful it is. It is pearl like, a gradient of gentle colors, tender pink, to soft blue, to an iridescent white. It looks soft, but its hardened beauty protects. Today's talk is so inspiring that Annie jots down notes. This is a good thing because ever since last night, she has had difficulty clearing her mind. Her first *To Do* item, Pete's crap and last night's heated exchange, has paralyzed her. Dr. Lisa breaks for a commercial and the incident replays itself. *It bothers Annie!* She wishes she would have governed her tongue and not been so direct. There is regret, just a touch. She knows that there are many other paths she could have taken, but didn't. She could have lifted Tom, inspired him. She should have said and done the things that build in him the same confidence she projects. Annie knows that this is both exactly what Tom needs and the very thing she usually provides, but last night it didn't happen. Pete pushes Tom around and Tom allows it, just lets him do it! To Annie this is so frustrating that sometimes her self-control disappears.

When Frank and Aggie retired and made their move, she'd hoped that maybe things would change, that maybe the distance between Lake Pulaski and Sanibel would break the spell and Tom would come into his own. Of course Pete is as haughty and overbearing as their father and Tom just rolls over and plays dead. Sometimes Annie wishes he could be more like her. She'd love to see him approach Pete the way he first pursued her. Back when they first met, he tossed all caution to the wind. He was willing to make a complete fool of himself simply for the opportunity to take her for a movie, a dinner, a dance, a lifetime. She'd never met anyone who was that self certain and she loved him for it.

This is what she finds *so* irritating. Annie shoots the refrigerator a stern glance and talks to it. "Why can't you be that confident with your family? It isn't difficult. You don't have to be disrespectful, just firm." She offers a dramatic pause and stares down the ice dispenser. "Just do a man to man with Pete; make it clear that despite your positions at the bank, there is an equal ground between the two of you and that you, Thomas James Hyden, expect to be treated with the kind of respect due a brother."

Frank,
> Pete,
>> Tom.

When it comes to this nonsense Annie's not sure which one ticks her off the most.

Just then she hears Tom's leather shoes clipping against the hallway tiles and remembers Dr. Lisa's words, *anger unbridled leads to a stampede.* She centers herself, throttles the temper, and waits to see him round the corner.

"Good morning honey." She smiles, hops off the stool, drapes her arms over his shoulders. "Sleep well?"

Sweet,
> positive,
>> convincing,

Annie dials back the emotion. She is so good at it that in the moment even she forgets all that lay beneath.

With his own easy way, Tom returns her smile, "A little tossing."

He pauses...turns a more serious tone "Annie, about last night..."

With pure contrition, Annie stops him, "Don't say another word, honey. That was all my fault. Sometimes I just can't help myself. Got to defend the man I love and I'd give anything if I could help you get Pete off your back."

Now Annie pauses... "I know you've got it in you, sweetheart. Remember how you chased after me...when we were dating how you wouldn't take no for an answer?"

"I think you've got that backwards, dear." Tom grins, "You were the one chasing me."

"Oh you..." Annie giggles and ever so playfully pushes against him. That action produces a reaction, Tom tightening his arms about her waist. "Think you're so funny..."

Just then Sophie shuffles around the corner and catches the mock struggle. "Oooo," she says, "Daddy loves mommy." Sophie might look like her mother, but she has adopted her father's art of the tease.

She is her usual morning mess, a look she wears with a comic's pride. On the left side of her part, her hair stands straight up. Over her shoulders, a pink robe twists. It is untied, exposing a women's tee so big it fits more like a night shirt. Sophie deals out hugs and takes her usual place, the island and the middle bar stool, where Annie has a glass of milk and a slice of peanut butter toast waiting. She tips the glass, bottoms up, and takes a big drink. The milk leaves a white moustache, another of daddy's tricks.

"Nice hair," Tom returns the banter, "Bet it took you all night to get it that perfect." Without cracking a smile, Sophie rocks her head, up once, down once.

Normally Annie would stand behind Sophie and run a brush through "the rat's nest". Normally this is a battle. Today she decides otherwise. Sophie and her father are on such a roll that any remaining tension is completely forgotten. It isn't often that this kind of misdirection happens and Annie instinctively knows that she'd be crazy to interrupt. With rare delight, the rest of the morning bounces and this makes everyone happy.

Truth be told, Annie adores her husband and finds few things more satisfying than displacing his doldrums. Today is especially pleasing. She kisses Tom goodbye and sends Sophie down the hall where Sophie's toothbrush is waiting and school clothes are already laid out.

As she picks up the kitchen, Annie notices that beneath the tea kettle the burner is still lit. She stops, studies it, slowly rotates the knob. The delicate lace grows, its intensity rising until the blue flame licks up and around the kettle's stainless steel edge. The pot shutters and the water inside begins a slow roll. She twists the knob back. The expected response is immediate.

Annie smiles, satisfied. "Adjust the heat to any level and there's no lag time, no warming up or cooling down. You get exactly what you ask for, exactly when you ask for it. "

This is why she had Tom install gas.

Chapter 8

JEN WEDGES HER INDEX FINGER between two slats and lifts slightly, creating a thin opening that runs almost the width of the mini blind. The gap is just enough. She watches as Joe's red pickup rolls out of the driveway.

The truck rounds the corner and she takes a deep breath. Is it relief or resignation? Either way it probably doesn't matter. Now that he is gone there is just one more stop before the day can begin, the bedroom where her phone is charging.

It is the second time this month she calls in sick.

Jen has another man. His name is Jack. Jack makes her feel good because, in fact, Jack makes her feel nothing at all. It has been hours since they were last together and the clarity that his absence creates paralyzes her. She walks through the kitchen and talks into the phone. She tells her boss that there is a heaviness in her chest, which is not a lie. Then out of his hiding place Jack appears. Lately the two of them have spent more time together, stealing a dull, passionless moment whenever they can. Does she love him? Does she hate him? She cannot say. All she knows for certain is that she needs him.

In this respect Jack is the perfect lover, expecting so little and promising so much. At the kitchen table, the two of them sit, and one sip at a time share their guilt free company. With Jack she doesn't have to explain herself or listen as he challenges her. She doesn't have to endure the impassioned pleas to "consider our life together" or "think about your wellbeing." Jack doesn't care about such things and this makes him the ideal companion. Into her emptiness, he pours himself, covering it with his sweet, pungent, golden nothing. Jen feels him inside her. She turns her head. The room slightly twists. She strains and listens for his silence. It sounds something like a cassette tape on which nothing is recorded. The metallic hiss is almost undetectable, yet it *is* there, providing just enough background noise. It removes her edginess. She talks to him. He doesn't talk back. Jack is, after all, not a conversationalist, just a disinterested lover who listens, listens, listens...

...or not. If she doesn't feel like talking, which is most of the time, his metallic silence keeps her company.

Indeed, silence is why she has turned to him.

Without Jack, silence sits like a mule. Its weight presses upon her chest and makes her listen to all the things she does not want to hear. Wedding vows, and fights, and lovemaking, life that was good, life as it should be, but isn't, silence makes her listen. Screaming doctors, frantic nurses bumping into stirrups, bloodied forceps chattering across metal trays, Joey's desperate gasping, there is so much that she doesn't want to hear, and that silence, that awful silence makes her listen.

Joey...

His deep eyes go dim, his beating heart stops; of all that silence forces upon her, this is the most unbearable. How long has it been? A year? Two? Pain makes time stand still. It fills silence's emptiness, reminding her that there are more ways to hurt than, before Joey, she would never have believed possible. This pain is sharp and dull, acute and chronic, a throbbing that sobs and an ache that cannot. Of course all of it, every bit of it reaches deep within her, rubbing raw her bruised and disfigured heart.

Silence? It never is. Without Jack, silence is just a dark cavern through which pain's awful noise echoes. It stubbornly pins her down. It *forces* her to listen. So she covets Jack and their time together alone. She waits, watching the red truck as it rounds the corner and disappears. She creates errands. "Joe, will you pick up some milk? Joe we're out of dish soap." His very presence demands of her that which she cannot give. Feeling. Loving. Caring. Passion. It hurts too much! So she waits. She sends Joe away or eventually he just leaves. Out comes her lover. Does he know about Jack? She is not sure. It's gotten so that she doesn't care.

Jack touches her lips and makes his loveless love. She swallows his flaccid disinterest, turns her head. Twisting becomes distortion. Clarity evaporates. The tape hisses louder, louder, louder, until it whites out pain's echoes. The mule gets up. Metallic silence fills the void.

Nothing feels good.

Chapter 9

U<small>P AND DOWN, OVER AND</small> around, Iowa's Black Sea swells, crests, falls. It looks fluid, moving, tide-like, but is not. The gentle undulations are, in fact, frozen, perpetually suspended. Time does not affect them. Hills that a hundred years ago rolled, still roll. Fields that for generations dipped and rose, remain gracefully, eternally fixed. The land never changes...

...or so it seems, until, that is, one notices the fence lines. Those lines, set decades ago, tell a different story. There was a day when field and fence were level. Now the ground on which those posts are set stand two, even three feet above the field. The fence lines have inadvertently become rulers measuring a different kind of movement. Wind blows. Snow melts. Water runs. Time passes. Weeks turn to months, months to years, years to decades. Soil secretly shifts, displaces, altogether disappears. To the naked eye, nothing changes. Unseen, yet constant, everything dissolves. The Black Sea recedes, the entire world disintegrates and without the fence lines, no one would ever know.

Today, Tom drives a familiar stretch and does not notice the rulers. He is going to Minneapolis, attending his bimonthly banker's meeting. There are more efficient routes; interstates that plot straight lines and shave down the travel time. Instead he chooses this, an old highway that winds in and among the swells. He looks ahead, sees beyond one curve and onto the next, and the next, and the next. He knows every rise, every trough. Like an old friend, the sea folds around him and even though it is a route he has taken hundreds of times, Tom finds it always interesting, always new.

The cell phone rings. On the display, a picture of his mother appears.

Just a couple of months after Frank's retirement and Pete's appointment, Aggie made another announcement. Frank had been diagnosed with dementia. The timing made Tom wonder. Frank stepped down, made Pete the new bank president. Aggie found a Sanibel real estate agent, sight unseen bought a beach house, packed everything they owned, made the move. Now this. Tom wondered, whether the dementia was a surprise or was it the reason they put their affairs in order and left town? According to Aggie this was not the retirement they'd planned. She claims that when the doctor broke the news she wanted to move back, she wanted her sons near. Of course, Frank wouldn't hear of it. If he was going to lose his memory and with it his dignity, Lake Pulaski would not be a witness.

At first, the dementia progressed slowly. Between the meds and Frank's finely honed social skills, his ailment was nearly unnoticeable. Only their closest friends knew and even they saw only rare glimpses. Time, of course, changes everything. Days turn to weeks, weeks to months, months to years. The world secretly shifts and this last stretch has been particularly hard. Frank now requires constant supervision, a job that is running Aggie ragged.

Tom looks at the picture, takes the call.

"Hi Mom. How'r you doin'?"

Aggie takes no time for pleasantries. Her voice carries desperation. "Tom, it's getting worse. I'm all by myself down here and don't know how much longer I can do this. I've got to watch him all the time. I'm afraid he's going to walk off, head down the beach and never find his way back home. I can't ever let him out of my sight. And you know how ornery he can be. He's been belligerent. I can't control him. I don't know what to do, Tom. I don't..."

"Jeez mom. Why don't you come home, bring him home. Annie and I will help you take care of him."

"It's too late for that, Tom. Moving back will confuse him even more than he already is. I don't think I have any choice. We must stay here... Besides, people around here are beginning to figure it out. If we were to move back to Lake Pulaski...Oh, I can only imagine... There'd be no hiding this. People will know."

"Maybe it's time they do know, mom."

Aggie lets the comment pass. There is a short, but heavy silence, a lag that Aggie immediately notices and fills.

"I wish Pete would call."

"I'll mention it to him, OK mom?"

"OK."

"Hey, is dad in the room with you? Why don't you put him on."

Tom hears Aggie's hand cover the phone. She says something that Tom cannot hear. She pauses, says something else, uncovers the phone.

"Hello? Is this Pete?"

"No dad. It's Tom."

"Oh Tom. How are you, son?"

"I'm fine dad, just fine."

"Do you remember back, way back? You were a...a uh...a junior crossing guard."

"Yes dad, I remember."

"Still have that picture from the paper. It's hanging in my office...How's Kelly?"

"You mean Annie, right dad?"

"Isn't this Pete?"

"No dad, it's Tom."

"Oh, Tom. How are you, son?"

"Fine dad."

"Do you remember back, way back? You were a...a uh..."

...a junior crossing guard. It was 5th grade and Tom was selected, one of only twelve. He passed the training and was fitted with the uniform, a yellow safety vest and his own Junior Crossing Guard badge. The daily assignments varied, raising the flag, policing the playground, or, of course, manning an intersection where he would stop traffic and safely usher the younger children across the street.

Early that fall, the Lake Pulaski Daily ran a feature story and Tom was chosen for the photo shoot. The picture was staged. Wearing vest and badge, a vigilant Tom gauged the traffic. Behind his outstretched arms stood several small children. The caption read, *"Junior Crossing Guard Keeps Youngsters Safe"*.

Frank was proud. He called the Daily and secured a glossy which he hung in his office. It was like a centerpiece and the only of Tom's accomplishments that ever received his father's attention. Pete's accolades were, of course, everywhere. Pete's four varsity football letters, Pete's 469 yard game, Pete's first team all-conference appointment, Pete's heroics as he led Lake Pulaski's state tournament run, these were all prominently displayed, but this, the Junior Crossing Guard, was the only visible acknowledgment that Frank had a second son.

It was later that year, the first snowfall. It was a wet snow, the kind out of which perfect snowballs are made. Tom was tending an intersection when one of the boys, another 5th grader, ambushed him. A tightly packed snowball exploded against Tom's head. Instinctively Tom returned fire, once, twice, three times.

To this day, Tom does not know if Mrs. Erickson, the school principal, saw the first snowball fly. If she did see it, if she saw that Tom was defending himself, then evidently she didn't care. All that mattered was that one of her Crossing Guards had shamed his uniform. She called Tom into her office. She issued punishment. "You will spend one recess on the playground," her voice was firm and matter of fact, "you will wear your vest and badge, and you will hold out your arms as though you are protecting children. You will show your classmates how a Junior Crossing Guard ought to behave.

That afternoon Tom resigned.

All those years, through grade school, middle school, and high school, even college, the newspaper glossy hung upon Frank's wall. It was Frank's conversation piece and his pride's only outward sign.

Tom never told his father...

"Do you remember back, way back? You were a...a uh...a junior crossing guard."

"Yes dad, I remember."

"Still have that picture from the paper. It's hanging in my office...How's Kelly?"

"You mean Annie, right dad?"

"Isn't this Pete?"

~ Rapture of the Deep ~

...Over 2,000 years ago a mathematician named Archimedes set forth this principle: "A buoyant force is equal to the weight of the displaced water"...In other words, if a diver weighs more than the water he is displacing, that diver will sink. If a diver weighs less than the water he is displacing, that diver will float. If a diver weighs the same as the water he is displacing he will neither sink nor float. This third state, neither sinking or floating, is called neutral buoyancy and when attained gives the diver a sense of complete weightlessness...A divers ability to manage the combination of weight and air necessary to achieve neutral buoyancy is called buoyancy control.

Open Water SCUBA Certification Manual
Compiled by DII (Dive Instructors International)
Pg. 37

Chapter 10

(A year and two months before the accident)

Account	Loan	Interest	Min Pmt Due	Pmt Rec'd
Pulaski Chevrolet	$521,056	2.99%	$1,298.30	$1,298.30
Frank Rich Tires	$382,121	3.125%	$995.11	$3,380.00
Bucholtz Contracting	$271,340	2.9%	$655.74	$655.74
Jensen Farms	$246,368	3.1125%	$641.58	

White
Gray
White
Gray

Beside the computer monitor sit checks, two piles. One pile is right side up, the other right side down. On the right side up pile,

Tom places his left hand, his three middle fingers underlining the amount. Over a numeric keypad his right hand floats. On the monitor, numbers appear, exact replicas of those written on the check. The check is then flipped, one pile to the other. The process repeats itself.

 Again.

  Again.

   Again.

 Behind every check is a story. Roy Jensen buys seed for spring planting, fuel for tractors, anhydrous to be knifed into the ground, parts for repair, but doesn't get paid until October's harvest is loaded on the semi and hauled to the elevator. Jerry Miller, the owner of Pulaski Chevrolet, fills the lot with new vehicles; trucks, cars, and vans that will take weeks, even months to sell. Mark Bucholtz Contracting builds spec homes. He hires a crew, pays subcontractors, rents equipment, pours footings, orders materials, knowing that only when the finished house is sold will he see a return. Some are short and some are long, but when it comes to money making pursuits, everything has a cycle, complete with a space of time between the cost of doing business and payday. Cash is Main Street's lubricant and precious few businesses are blessed with its steady, regular flow.

 Enter the bank and its oil can called the operating loan, a short term credit line that puts seed in the ground, keeps Chevys rolling onto the lot, gives Mr. Bucholtz something to nail together. The monthly installments are small. These "interest only" minimums come with the promise that when "the business gets paid, the bank gets paid." So, for instance, Roy Jensen pays his $641.58 monthly minimum. This is only interest; rent on the cash he's using. When harvest comes or the corn market rises, he sells a load of corn or beans, writes the bank a fat check, and pays down the loan.

Account	Loan	Interest	Min Pmt Due	Pmt Rec'd
Ranchers Supply	$119,285	3.125%	$310.64	$16,380.00
Heartland Excavating	$670,940	2.9%	$1,621.44	$41,271.44

The cell phone rings and breaks Tom's concentration. He looks. The display tells him that *Unknown Number* is calling. He does not answer. Actually, the number is not completely unknown. It could be one of many numbers; First Bank Visa, Central Bank Visa, or his Discover card. Lately even the gas and electric company has been calling. At least a couple times a week *Unknown Number* checks in.

"Mr. Hyden, this is Candy from Discover."

"This is Rob from First Bank."

"This is Rita from Iowa Power and Light."

"I need to speak with you about your account."

"I see you've missed your recent payment.

I'm sure it was an oversight.

Please call so we can get you up to date."

"Your account is seriously delinquent.

Call to avoid further action."

Tom never takes *Unknown Number's* call. Always they will leave a message. Most of the time he will listen. Sometimes he calls back.

Today he will not. With a $182.64 checking account balance, returning the call is pointless. *Unknown Number* will have to wait until Wednesday, payday, and the next time he unlocks the roll top.

Still, the call chills him. He finds his ledge and refocuses; the computer monitor, the two piles, the numeric keypad, the exact replicas.

"Where was I?...Heartland Excavating, $41,271.44."

Tom studies the glowing monitor and realizes that something isn't quite right. He examines the check, rereads the number, $41,721.44, catches the mistake, repositions the curser, and begins making the correction.

Tom pauses, "A 2 to a 7, a 7 to a 2, and a $450 shortfall that I won't have to find when I reconcile today's business." He looks at the error again. "Transposing numbers, a common mistake. Happens all the time."

450. Coincidently this is almost exactly the amount that Tom owes Iowa Power.

For a moment, and just for a moment Tom considers his business, the lending business. He thinks about how he might expand that business, how he might open his own personal bank, how he might silently weave the numbers beneath his roll top into these gray and white rows. Such a weaving might fence the Rottweilers, might even pull their teeth. He studies the ledger, its thin columns, its shaded gray lines, and sees all the entries that could more than cover minimum payments. There are so many.

"I'd call it Bank of Tom." The idea makes him smile. "Do it right and Heartland Excavating would never notice. Borrow 450 now. Heartland's minimum payment is more than satisfied. There would be no notices generated, no fees or penalties incurred." He knows Gladys, Heartland Excavating's bookkeeper. "Hell, she's so busy that she'd never check things that closely and never bother looking online. Before her next statement cycles, I borrow from someone else, pay Heartland back, and no one's the wiser."

The possibilities unfold. Tom sees a giant tree, in every direction transactions branching. Borrowing from one, paying another, it's intricate, beautiful, and all so simple that he almost forgets to ask himself the obvious question. "Is it stealing if everyone always gets paid?" Of course in that single moment, the answer is as obvious as the question. "No, it's an operating loan and nobody gets hurt."

Just then a dark void settles upon him. It is deeper and darker than the emptiness beneath the other night's balance beam. He sees the memo pad that sits upon his desk, notices the heading "Lakeland Savings and Trust". He glances up and studies pictures, Annie and Sophie and their deeply searching eyes. In their own way, they both need him. He returns their loving gaze and promises his protection.

"I am an honest man." In a shame that only he can see, Tom lowers his eyes. Never has such a thought entered his head. Quickly, almost clandestinely, he fixes the ledger.

That night he lies in his bed and stares at a ceiling fan that, for the darkness, cannot be seen. There is no first sleep. There is no ledge and no Rottweilers. There is not even a drift. There is only a lightless, empty shame.

Chapter 11

He measures, floor to the top of the door leaving a quarter inch reveal.

82 ³⁄₈ Ssssssshetd. The measuring tape sucks back into its housing.

On the miter table a length of maple casing lay. Over it, Joe stretches the tape.

82 ³⁄₈

He makes a mark, Ssssssshetd. He pushes the casing flush against the fence and lowers the unengaged blade until it nearly touches the wood. Gently, he taps the casing, right and then a little left, until the pencil mark and the edge of the blade are aligned. The saw spins to life. White dust flies, producing a perfectly clean 45 degree edge. He studies the piece. Three thin brown lines randomly arch across a nearly white surface. Toward and away from each other they bend, but never intersect.

Against the wall Joe leans the finished piece. Over the other side of the jamb, he extends his tape. He thinks about Jen. Lately she is all he can think about. He can't explain it, but something is happening, something dark, haunting. He so wants this something to disappear, but it won't. He so wants to apply his calm, steady nature hoping that the something might be tamed, but it will not cooperate.

82 3/8

82 3/8 Mark. Tap. Cut. Study...

In a carpenter's world, there are two kinds of beauty. One is *a gift,* a force of nature that can only be recognized for what it is.

The other is *a skill* to be honed.

When he first noticed *the gift,* Joe was just a boy, not much older than Sophie. It was a Sunday morning, which was a good thing, since nearly everyone was still in church. Pastor Gormally was finishing a lengthy exposition, Jesus calming the seas, when the storm sirens wailed and the twister clobbered the other side of town. Of course, some thought the timing providence. Joe's father called it "long winded luck". In any event, the storm unleashed a fury that leveled two dozen homes, damaged sixty others, and brought down hundreds of trees, including the old ash that graced the Johnson back yard.

The tree was a stately giant, over forty feet tall and seemingly invincible. After the storm, it lay on its side looking like a fallen general and leaving a hole in the sky above the place where it once stood. For the first time in decades, sunlight bathed every corner of the yard, which on that particular day was as harsh as the storm it followed.

Clean up took over a week. Men in hard hats came. Their chain saws whined, reducing the giant into three neatly stacked piles; small branches that held the leaves, limbs on which those branches were once attached, and finally slices of the trunk.

It was one of these cross sections, a piece from near the base that caught Joe's eye. The thing was over two and a half feet in diameter. It stood on its bark lined edge and looked something like a rolling barrel on which circus elephants might balance themselves. Joe leaned against the trunk; tried tipping the thing over, but the weight was such that there was no moving it. So he found Tom and together the two of them pushed until the piece toppled, and the barrel became a table top.

The boys inspected their find. Concentric rings swept around and spiraled downward, forming a tunnel through which would-be travelers might pass. One world to another, the passage had a feeling of inevitability, of direction and purpose, yet there was also a randomness to it. In its own unique way, each ring moved; light into dark, wide and narrow, regular and irregular, none perfectly circular, yet every one so distinct that from the outside, all the way down to the pith, each ring could be numbered. Seeing it was almost dizzying and formed a three dimensional illusion, a corkscrewed time machine.

It didn't take long and Tom grew tired of this new toy. Joe, on the other hand, could not take his eyes off it. It was, to him, the most mysteriously beautiful thing he'd ever seen.

"Com' on, Puck. Let's find the guys, see if anyone wants to play some work-up."

"Sure Hyden." Over the end of his handle bar Joe slipped his ball glove, mounted his bike, and glanced back. Beneath the hot sun the table top shined.

That evening Joe parked himself beside the trunk.

His father, who relished such opportunities, came and sat beside Joe. He had always been attentive, but now even more so. It had been eight months since her death and he knew how much Joe needed his mother. If losing his wife had been hard on him, he didn't show it, at least not to Joe.

"Every ring is a year," his father stated, "and every ring holds its own story."

"Look here," his father extended a finger and touched a wide, blond band, "Can't say for certain, but I'll bet this was a springtime so perfect, that it brought with it an inch of new growth." He moved his finger, touched a dark, heavy line. "Maybe a blistering summer, such heat that all the tree could manage was this thin, dense growth. Years of health, years of disease. Years of ease and years of stress." His dad paused. "How did it get that way? Only the tree knows for sure and it's not talking."

Of course for Joe, this explanation only intensified the wonder. Imagine, a trove of secret stories set deep beneath this hidden labyrinth, an absolute beauty, layer after layer wrapped in its own crusty protection. How could anything be more perfect?

In a comfortable silence, the two of them sat and watched daylight fade. Joe lay back, resting his head upon his father's lap. Into those kind, dark eyes he gazed, taking note of the lines around those eyes and how the years had deepened them. With his index finger he reached up and gently traced the circles, wondering what stories they kept, how the unspoken sorrow of losing his wife and the quiet trial of now raising a son by himself might have shaped this graceful flow. The sun set. As it did, the open space left by the fallen ash filled itself. Stars, countless in number, formed a garland about his father's head. Oh how Joe loved this man, how he hoped that someday he could be to his own son what his dad was to him.

After that evening Joe saw things differently. Every tree became a hidden beauty, every piece of wood a book containing enigmatic codes, every person a trunk the depth and wonder of which could never be completely plumed. The world was a new place and Joe had a tornado, his father, and that uprooted ash to thank for it.

Later that week, just before the hard hats fed the tree into the chipper, Joe and his father rescued several large limbs and stored them behind the shed. Joe's dad thought he'd cure the wood and use it for bonfires. Joe had another plan. He decided he'd learn everything he could about these branches. He stripped bark. He cut lengthwise cross sections, hoping that he might see the growth rings flow in ways other than the circles with which he'd become familiar. He uncovered grain, sanded smooth rough edges, applied clear coat finishes so that, with a peacock's pride, those ovals strutted around the boards. This first beauty, this *gift to be admired*, so inspired him that he pursued the second beauty and learned the woodworker's *skill*. By the time he'd graduated from high school, Joe was a self-taught craftsman, and a good one at that. Before he finished carpentry school the community college offered him a teaching position. Joe turned it down, preferring instead to unwrap the forest, reveal its cryptic stories, and fill Lake Pulaski's homes with its graceful enigmas. Every piece of every table, of every chair, of every cabinet was both a seamless fit and a testament to the trees from which they were fashioned.

It was his fascination with deeply hidden stories that drew him to Jen. From the moment she sent that baseball whistling over everyone's heads he knew that somewhere inside this girl lay a wonderfully mysterious paradox.

On the outside, she presented herself as a force of nature, tough, ornery, edgy, abrasive, and volatile. This, of course, was all a pretense, Jen's protective bark, and no one saw beneath it, no one, that is, except Joe. He looked right through her crusty exterior and saw something so delicate and so fragile that he had to know more. With an inexplicable softness, her hard edges curved and Joe constantly found himself wondering how those fiery eyes could possess the same kindness he saw in his father's. Everything about this girl was a contradiction, and he wanted to know all there was to know. He wanted to spend a lifetime unwrapping the spirals, understanding the restlessly moving lines, exploring that corkscrewed tunnel with its deeply embedded mysteries.

Over time, Joe began to understand that Jen's temper was *his* gateway, and that if he really wanted to discover what it was that made her tick he'd have to do two things, piss her off and hang on! So he did. He teased, he taunted, he tormented and she kept coming back, wanting more. It was such an exquisite irony. The same anger that kept the world at arm's length was Joe's entry point. To most, it was a locked door, forbidden territory. For him? It was a key granting entrance. This was, to be sure, a privileged access and with it a dual purpose developed. Incite anger, watch the story unfold. Only to Joe were her secrets made known and the passionate dance that produced these revelations also forged an intense and trusting intimacy.

Getting to it took only a nudge. Often he didn't even have to know what to nudge, or where. He just had to nudge. Then came the twister, an anger that with unbridled fury whipped, which he not only took, but with equal intensity, returned to her. So the storm would rage until everything was stripped bare and they stood before each other with nothing between them but the truth of who they were. All the veils were lifted. There was no pretending that all was well, no holding back, no fear of being vulnerable or worrying that one might hurt the other. It was like Adam and Eve for the very first time laying eyes upon each other. Every storm left the two of them naked and unashamed.

In the end, it was not the fight that he loved, but what the fight did. It was not the anger that moved him, but the fact that the anger had a point, a driving purpose as clear, as pristine as an ocean current. Anger and argument were merely the tools of Joe's love and he used them whenever he felt Jen retreating into her protective shell or sensed that she was afraid and concealing some angst or hurt.

So one by one the growth lines appeared. So one by one she dropped her defenses. So one by one she placed these fragile mysteries into his care. This was how she came to tell Joe everything, her hurt when a new girlfriend dumped her, the guilt over her parents' divorce, her uncle Terry.

Uncle Terry... a line darker than all the others yet so thinly disgraceful that it was nearly invisible. In fact, they were four and a half years into married life before Joe made the discovery and even then he had to stumble upon it. It appeared one evening while they were out with the Hydens. The four of them met at Sparky's. They were sitting in a booth sharing a pitcher and planning their next vacation when Joe reached over, slid his hand just inside Jen's knee, and gently rubbed. The gesture held no motive other than Joe's usual demonstration of his affection, yet Jen's response was instinctive, visceral, like that of a wounded animal. With a single motion, she pushed her knees together, grabbed Joe's wrist, and tossed his hand aside. Joe was stunned, but didn't let on. If the Hydens saw what had happened, they both pretended otherwise.

He waited. They said their goodbyes, got into his truck, closed the doors. "What the hell was that all about?"

"Keep your hands to yourself, you horny..."

"Horny? I meant nothing of the sort. I've touched you a thousand times before and you've never minded. What's going on???"

Silence...Over the pickup, in the garage, through the house, that silence hung.

"Jen?" Up the stairs, into the bedroom, he followed her.

"Butt out!" She peeled her jeans down around her ankles then kicked them at the hamper.

Joe placed himself between Jen and the closet, blocking the path to her night shirts.

"No! Not until you tell me what's going on."

"It's nothing."

"Bullshit! I saw your eyes. You were scared to death...Still are."

With a fury the likes of which Joe had never before seen, this storm blew. It lasted nearly an hour and left Jen heaped upon the floor. Through sobs that rose and fell like ocean tides Joe could just barely hear it. "I couldn't stop him... I... I tried... I... couldn't... Why... couldn't I? Why? Why? Why?"

Out it came. She was only twelve when it first happened. Uncle Terry had always been affectionate, so much like a father should be and so unlike her father was. With her parents stuck in the mire of their sinking marriage, Terry's attentiveness was just about the only bright spot in her otherwise drab world and she trusted him.

At the dinner table one night it happened. She remembered, at first, thinking it odd, odd that Uncle Terry would secretly slide his hand over her knee. It was such an unexpected touch, not a gentle pat, not his usual signal of endearment. No. The hand stayed, motionless, heavy. It was there so long that beneath it a warmth developed yet its invasive presence chilled her. Then the hand moved, working its way inside her knee and up slightly. Jen froze. She wanted to pick up the hand like one would pick up a piece of rancid garbage. She wanted to drop it on Uncle Terry's plate, show everyone, but she didn't. She couldn't, and the inability to expose this unwelcome thing that stroked the inside of her thigh made Jen feel dirty.

For the next three years, he molested her: Three years of "Don't tell anyone". Three years keeping a fear filled watch, never knowing when he would pin her against the bed or trap her behind the bathroom door. Three years of secrets that evolved, becoming a lifetime of concealed shame.

The story spilled out of her, its ugliness flooding the room. When it was done, Jen curled into a fetal ball, making herself thin, nearly invisible, but no matter how small she made herself, it wasn't enough. Nothing could hide this. So she lay there in the only way she could, shamefully exposed, the salt from drying tears and evaporating sweat leaving a gritty, humiliating stench that stuck to her shoulders, her arm pits, her torso.

It's funny. How is it that two people can look at exactly the same thing and see that thing so differently? Where Tom saw an ash trunk toppled by a twister, Joe saw a veiled wonder. Where over the years, the many friends Jen burned through saw unstable anger, she saw wounds needing her protection. Where Jen saw a weak and worthless piece of crap, Uncle Terry's sub-human toilet, Joe saw a creature lovely and noble, a perfect beauty formed of the random lines that inevitably emerge when pathos begets perseverance, when a world malevolent and ugly inexplicably produces undaunted hope, an audacious spirit.

Joe stripped away his tee shirt and folded himself around her, his lips so close to her ear that the sounds they made as he formed words were louder than the words themselves.

"You're so hard headed. Why do you insist on going it alone? Don't ever do this alone..."

"Hold me, Joe..." Her voice quivered, nearly broke. "Hold me..."

She laid her palm over the back of his hand, gently inserting her thin fingers into the creases between his knuckles. Intertwined, she guided his hand onto her knee, released her grip, and ever so delicately pushed his fingers directly over the place of violation. His hand was not heavy. His hand was cool, medicinal, like that of a menthol salve.

"Hold me Joe...Hold me..."

He did. He held her until they both fell asleep. All night long they lay beside their still made bed, salt against salt, a stickiness that first fused them into a single, living being then turned cool, cool like the hand that cradled her injury. The sleep was so deep, so perfect, so restful that only a sliver of mid-morning sun would raise them from their slumber.

~~~~~~

32 ¼.

32 ¼. Mark. Tap. Cut. Study...

It all seems so long ago. Now? Now she wears so many layers that Joe doesn't know where to begin. In fact, he's not even sure if beneath those layers there's anything left. Maybe Jen's whiskey soaked spirit has reduced her into a protective layer with nothing to protect. Maybe these last couple of years and their terrible events have somehow dissolved her mysteriously sweeping essence and turned to mush that once darkly beautiful core. He doesn't know.

The thought is black as night and it scares him. He begins to feel something that he has never felt before. At first it feels something like anger, like the anger they used to feel for each other when the two of them cared enough to fight, but it is not that. That anger was clear, purposeful. No, this is not anger. This is more like futility, a deep, bottomless futility. This is more like nothing, no purpose, no reason, just the loss of everything he holds dear. First, it was mom, next it was dad, then Joey. Now he watches helplessly as Jen slips away, and he knows that this is a loss he cannot bear.

He goes through the motions, pushing the freshly cut casing against the top of the door frame. He eyeballs the Reveal. Cha-cu. Cha-cu... Cha-cu. The compressor chugs to life. Joe sets down the nail gun and dry fits the next piece, a length of casing that will soon cover the right side of the frame.

It doesn't matter. Nothing does; not the nearly white surface, not the free flowing lines, or the path they travel, or the stories they keep. It doesn't matter.

Everything is black.

Chapter 12

"Sssshhumpf." Inside Joe's BC[2], compressed air shoots, expands, creates a small pocket, and with it some needed lift.

He hangs, inhales, waits. He is testing his buoyancy, wondering if the air that now fills his lungs offsets his body weight.

It does not.

He again squeezes the inflator, button. "Sssshhumpf."

He hangs,
    inhales,
        waits.

This time there is a sensation, a slight rising, but still it is not quite right. "Sssshhumpf."

He breathes, slowly, naturally.
    In.
        Out.

---

2. A Buoyancy Compensator (BC) is an inflatable vest. This is an essential piece of equipment that helps divers control their underwater buoyancy. The vest also includes a strap (to secure the air tank), attachment rings (to secure dive gear), and pockets.

His body falls,
>rises.
Again he breathes.
>In...
>>falling.
>Out...
>>rising.

The motion is backward, counter intuitive. One would expect a body to act like a balloon, but it does not. Fill a balloon and immediately it rises. Release trapped air and immediately the container sinks. Diving doesn't work that way. It is more a delayed reaction, something like watching a movie in which voices and lips are not quite synced. In the same way, body weight and the inertia it creates delays nature's forces and produces an out of sync motion. As air fills the diver's lungs, the falling that has just begun continues. As that breath is released the rising that has just begun continues.

So it is, air arrests sinking, weight arrests floating. The two in proper combination find a perfect balance, and with the equilibrium comes a steady, gentle rocking, an unearthly underwater seesaw.

In...falling.
>Out...rising.
>>Weightlessness.

To Joe, it is a familiar, welcome, and grace filled ballet.

Divers call this buoyancy control, but it is not control, not really. No, it is more like relinquishing control. It is a mysterious, unseen force seeking his trust and to it Joe willingly surrenders.

He hovers,
>closes his eyes,
>>feels the ballet's serenity,
>>>and begins releasing all the other topside pressures.

Releasing pressures. This takes a few minutes.
Toes, feet, legs,
    fingers, hands, arms,
        torso, spine,
            neck, head,
    and all the muscles that support them:
It takes a few minutes.

This watery, weightless world is, after all, a foreign place, a place in which he is but a visitor. In it, the surface's ambient demands do not exist. Thus before his body will fully embrace water's gifts, it needs to adjust. It must forget where it has been and all that gravity imposes.

In...
    falling.
Out...
    rising.

It takes a few minutes, but when finally all is forgotten, when finally surrender is complete and the body is released, there comes upon Joe an unqualified peace.

    It confers an ethereal existence.
    It suspends the world as it is.
No muscles tensed.
    No limbs, no appendages, no digits tightened.
        No joints stressed.
            His body??? Completely at rest.
Here there is no sound,
    no wind rustling leaves,
        no rush of traffic,
            no voices of expectations
                or disappointments.
Here there is only the regulator's hiss,

only the plumping of bubbles as they form beneath
> his chin.

Here body, mind, spirit, everything is at ease.
> Everything is still.

It is an odd paradox. Weightlessness requires water's weight. Featherlike freedom forms in a liquid density. Erasing gravity's primal forces means that tons upon tons of water will squeeze him. In all directions, he will be squeezed and that squeezing removes every pressure.

It is indeed an odd paradox.

Joe opens his eyes, sees Tom who hangs beside him. A curious smallie[3] has already found them. She investigates and is *not* shy, placing herself directly in Tom's path. The two are nose to nose, barely two feet separates them. Tom fins forward. The smallie yields, then follows.

Today Eldo's Pond offers its usual visibility, a mere 8 feet. This is nothing like Cozumel and its current washed clarity, but seeing is not what brings them here. They are here to be weightless, free from gravity and its laws, free from the constant forces that push them into the ground.

So the morning unfolds. So the water embraces them. Its pressure removes all pressure. Its heavy demands make no demands. It has no memory and through its emerald brightness they lilt,
> lightly,
>> poetically,
>>> effortlessly.
> falling,
>> rising.
> falling,
>> rising.

---

3. Small Mouth Bass

As mentioned earlier, water is denser than air. This means that underwater everything changes, including what you see. First there is refraction. Fill a water glass and place a straw in that glass. When you do, you'll notice that the straw looks bent. The straw is, in fact, straight. It is light that is being bent... This bending magnifies everything. Underwater objects look larger and closer than they really are; 25% larger and closer. Thus that Goliath Grouper you see on one of your dives is not nearly as big as you think.

There is also something called light absorption. Because of water's density, the deeper you dive, the more light is absorbed. It begins with the longer wave lengths. At 15 feet red starts turning gray. Next it's orange (about 25 feet), then yellow (35 feet). At 50 feet green begins to fade, until at 100 feet only blue, Indigo, and violet are left.

Eventually everything becomes shades of gray.

Open Water SCUBA Certification Manual
Compiled by DII (Dive Instructors International)
Pg. 68

Chapter 13

(A year before the accident)

TOM DOESN'T KNOW WHEN EXACTLY the finances so dramatically tipped. There was no defining moment or single event that clearly marked the beginning. There was no one bill that hit his mail box or angry creditor urgently demanding "payment in full". There wasn't a roof that needed replacing or an unexpected emergency room visit. Neither was it braces for Sophie or a forgotten credit card that Annie loaded to the gills. No. The threat of imminent collapse just happened. It was as if Tom had been running a 10,000 meter race. Slowly, steadily he circled the track, hoping he could catch the leaders, put himself in the hunt, someday maybe even win the race. With all his strength he ran, only to now glance over his shoulder and discover that he is about to be lapped. The pursuer has become the pursued and Tom is no longer playing catchup. He is running for his life.

What's different than last week, three weeks ago, six weeks ago? He cannot say. All Tom knows is that everywhere he looks, he sees an impending crisis. One by one, bills have morphed into letters, legal teams and collection agencies giving their final notice. The calls from *Unknown Number* have increased six fold. His checking account tells him that the mortgage payment must wait until mid-month. Beneath the roll top, the stacks of "paid today", "paid next week", "paid next month" are all "on hold". The pack is closing the distance. He can't let them catch him. He can't be lapped. He quickens his pace. It is not enough. Never has he been this uncertain, *this* afraid.

The cell phone rings. Sophie's name and picture lights the screen. He clears his mind, mentally changes his tone. "Hey punkin'! Aren't you in school?"

"Yep. Sorry Daddy. I knooow. My cell phone is just for 'mergencies, but it's lunch time and I'm on the playground."

"It's ok. What's up?"

"Don't forget to come to my program this afternoon."

Tom's voice carries a mock urgency, "You have a program this afternoon?"

"DAA-DY!!!!!" Sophie delights. She loves the way he teases.

"I wouldn't miss it for the world, you know that sweetie. I'll be on time, 5:30."

"DAAAA-DY!!!!"

"I know, I know, 2:30. See you then..."

He closes his eyes, feels his smile fall.

"The mortgage..."

His heart sinks.

Tom again glances over his shoulder and sees the future that's chasing him. It will soon begin, when, at the end of the month, meeting minimums is longer possible. One, or probably two credit cards will be revoked. Next month's electric bill will come and will not get paid. Iowa Power will send a disconnect notice. *Annie cannot know.* To satisfy the utilities, he will miss a mortgage payment. A few weeks later, another card will shut down. He is drowning in minimums. One by one the pack catches him. As they draw near, he gets a better look. They are not runners. They are the Rottweilers, the same beasts that nightly visit his bedroom. They overtake him and as they do they nip his heals, draw a little blood, tear a little flesh. Another card will be cancelled. Somehow Pete will find out. He will call a meeting. The two of them will exchange words. Tom will be fired. Everything will be lost.

Tom has used all his tricks and unlike the middle of the night, there is no hiding. The ledge, that temporary safe place where, at one time, he'd sit and feed hungry dogs is gone. So many times he has juggled, sorted, talked, and promised, and while it wasn't pleasant, he always found a way, he always stayed ahead. Always. This time he can't and he knows it.

At his desk he sits, goes through the motions called work. He looks at the monitor and its neatly kept rows. He flips checks, one pile to the next. He pages through investment statements, balance sheets, valuation reports. He sees none of it.

Account	Loan	Interest	Min Pmt Due	Pmt Rec'd
Jensen Farms	$246,368	3.125%	$641.58	$641.58
Lakes Pulaski Lumber	$68,214	3.00%	$170.54	$170.54
Bucholtz Contracting	$271,340	2.9%	$655.74	$68,915.38

He stops, looks. Bucholtz's most recent payment, this number he sees. Of course he doesn't see the entire number, just the 9 and the 1...or is it a 1 and a 9? He isn't sure. He mouths the words, "I am in the lending business."

It has been over two months since he first considered the shameful thing and immediately dismissed it. The idea came back. Over and over again, it came back. He put it out of his mind, told himself that "never in a million years would he do something like this." The idea returned. He immersed himself, work, play, family time. He kept himself so occupied that the idea couldn't possibly grow. It grew anyway. It was like the foxtail barley lining railroad grades. Cut it, pull it, poison it, dig it up so that no trace remains, and the weed reappears, more noxious, more prolific than ever. So it has been, this last month. At the mail box, in the grocery store checkout line, gassing up the car, and especially each day coming to work and staring at that gray and white grid, the idea aggressively grew. Since he couldn't kill it, he tried living around it. He developed a plan and convinced himself it was a harmless daydream. He applied his love of detail and decided it was only a mental exercise. When it became a two part plan, a plan that completely covered his tracks, the idea's simplicity so frightened him that he pulled it, roots and all. In less than a day, it reappeared, more pernicious than before. Now here he is, seeing not a computer screen, but a door, a fix, a way out of the mess.

Around his temple, beads of cold sweat gather. Everything becomes a question.

"Am I in the lending business?"

"Am I an honest man?"

"Is it stealing if everyone gets paid?"

"No!" "Yes..."

He isn't sure...

He glances over his shoulder, sees what will be. He looks ahead, watches Annie and Sophie and how the impending crash shreds them. He sees Lake Pulaski's cruel propensity and the destruction it will bring. He sees hardship. He sees pain. He sees shame. Everything about this is *his* wrong, *his* fault! Annie. Sophie. He cannot, he *will not* let them be hurt!

He sees a 9 and a 1, wonders if it isn't a 1 and a 9. He truly does not know which is right.

He is so afraid.

Fear. There is, of course, the obvious fear, that of getting caught. While this prospect makes Tom's heart pound, there is something else, something large and formless, something he can't see, but knows is there and this knowing raises in him an indescribable dread. Since he can't see it, he cannot say exactly what it is, but believes it has something to do with the door his computer screen has become and the promised fix that lay just beyond its threshold. At first, he can't place it, but the door looks vaguely familiar, like another place he has visited.

Then he remembers...Eldo's Pond, an old limestone quarry that is now part of Miner's State Park. At a depth of 52 feet there sits an abandoned double-wide. Back in the day, the men that worked the mine used it as a check point. Finding that trailer was easy. Tom and Puck simply swam above the old road bed until there in the green water the thing materialized. Its windows were black and the door hung wide open, looking as though the last man out left in such a hurry that he forgot to lock up. Around this opening, the two divers hovered, their lights cutting through the black interior. While the room was dark, the water was remarkably clear. Just then Tom's beam caught something shiny. It flashed. He swept the light backward, retracing the beam's path. It flashed again. Was it a coin, a small fish, something else? He couldn't say, but the shiny something so piqued his interest that, for a moment, he forgot himself. With a single motion, Tom finned. Into that perfectly clear darkness he glided, following the curiosity that led him forward.

It was a spoon.

Tom examined his find, slid it into his BC, and turned toward an exit that was now gone. From under his fins, silt mushroomed. Before he knew what was happening, the brown cloud overtook then enveloped him so that there was no right, no left, no up, no down, and most of all no hope of finding the door. Fear escalated, became panic. "Panic kills!" This mantra, a part of every diver's training was for Tom so instinctive that he said it almost out loud. He fought back the anxiety, released a deep breath, reached for gauges he could only feel, and pressed the lit display against his mask. It told him that his tank contained 1400 pounds, under these conditions air enough for about 25 minutes. Tom became motionless, measured his breathing and with it his thought processes. The world became a slow motion movie. He remembered the room, the things in the room and the space between them. In his mind, he mapped every cabinet, every counter, every water-soaked office chair. He weighed his options, considered waiting and wondered if the silt would clear before his tank ran dry. Next he imagined feeling his way toward a file cabinet and using the furniture as a blind man's compass. Panic again rose. Again he fought it, relaxed his body, slowed his breathing.

Just then Tom felt something grab his wrist and saw a second light, its diffused beam bouncing through the brown sludge. The something led him. He followed. Puck, who watched the trailer door belch silt, tied a guide line, found his friend, and followed that line back to safety.

Some time later Tom heard about a diver who died this way, her body discovered a mere three feet from safe passage. *Three feet* and she couldn't find the exit! The thought still gives Tom shivers.

~~~~~~~~~~~~~~

Tom sits at his desk, seeing not a computer screen, but a door, a fix, a way out of one mess, but into another. This door, it is an enigma, a large, formless something and even though he can't see that mucky, brown layer as it rests undisturbed, as it hides beneath the dark blanket and its perfect clarity, he instinctively understands. Something dangerous eludes his sight. It is, after all, one thing to consider stealing, to devise a plan, map the details, run all the possible problems and fit those problems with their appropriate contingencies. It is quite another to actually steal and he passes over *that* threshold, unseen clouds will billow, the exits will disappear, and his world will become one shitty mess. When this happens, when the basis of self-respect, integrity, honor, everything that makes him what he is becomes hopelessly lost, the man known as Thomas James Hyden may no longer exist. Yes, getting caught is one thing, but this? This scares the hell out of him.

While in this precise moment, he can't see any details, this much he understands. He knows that this is why only a month ago stealing was unthinkable. He also understands that this is why such unthinkable actions, actions that change everything about one's life require unthinkable circumstances, circumstances so outweighing the action's consequence that the choice, to act or not to act, is really no choice at all.

These are, of course, matters currently hidden and the fear Tom feels rests beneath its large, ominous shroud. For now Tom hovers. Into a perfectly clear darkness, he shines his light and sees only that which his beam illuminates. He sees shame, failure, imminent demise, the loss of *everything*. He sees Annie suffering *his* humiliation. He sees Sophie and the painful discovery that her father, the only person in her life that she can completely trust, has failed her. This is the perfectly clear darkness that quickens his resolve; that removes his pause and propels him over that threshold. These are the unthinkable circumstances that send him toward a shiny something and into a room with no egress.

Tom pulls a little line from his dive reel, ties it on the door, and hopes it is well anchored. He then looks at the check from Bucholtz and very clearly sees a 1, a 9, and $720, his first operating loan.

"Transposed numbers, a common mistake."

He opens three different vendor accounts and makes entries.

Iowa Abstract	$177.31
Midwest Maid Cleaning Service	$268.15
Office Buddy (Office Supplies	$274.54
Total:	$720.00

From his desk drawer, he pulls three tickets and fills the blanks.

"Mr. Hyden."

He feels panic, just a bit,
    slows his breathing,
        without moving looks up.

"Mary. Yes. How may I help you?"

"I'm sorry to bother you, you look so busy."

He x'es out of the ledger. "It's ok. What do you need?"

"Mr. Johnson stopped by. At the time, you were with your brother and when you finished I forgot to mention it to you."

"That's fine, Mary. Puck and I are planning another weekend dive, he probably just wanted to shoot the breeze." Tom pauses, "While you're here, I'm just finishing these tickets. Will you take them to one of the tellers and have them cut the checks?"

"Sure Mr. Hyden."

Mary takes the tickets and leaves his office. Just then Tom realizes that he has not worked out the details. He's not completely sure how he will cash these checks, how he will mask his identity, or even where he will launder the funds. Panic rises. He breathes, relaxes, checks his gauges. For now, Tom has a couple of non-Lakeland Savings and Trust checking accounts. For now, the checks will go there. He will make deposits through ATMs. Everything will process electronically. No one will check his identity. No one will ask questions.

He waits. Mary does not return. 1:30. 1:47. 2:03. "Where is she?" In less than 20 minutes, Sophie's program will begin. Tom needs to leave…soon. He moves slowly, deliberately. He shuts down his computer, closes his office door, and steps up to Mary's desk.

"I'm heading out. Got to get to the school and hear Sophie sing. Did you get those checks cut?"

"Yes, Mr. Hyden. I put them in the outgoing mail."

A billowing cloud envelops him. Fear becomes a wave of panic. He wants to shout "YOU DID WHAT!" He wants to sprint for the mailbox. With every ounce of strength he fights it back, makes himself motionless, sets the world in slow motion, weighs his options.

"Mary, you are so good," he smiles the words, "I tell you, I've got the best office manager in Lake Pulaski."

"Why thank you, Mr. Hyden."

Tom relaxes, further slows his breathing, and moves toward the exit. Before leaving he makes two stops, first the bathroom and then beside it, the mail room. The outbox is still full. The mailman has not yet come. He releases a deep breath, sorts through the envelopes, and pulls his loan checks.

As he walks toward his car, he tells himself. "I'll pay it back." He knows that because he can't, he won't. He thinks it anyway.

Tom arrives first and saves Annie a seat. He has read that for some people stealing brings with it a certain thrill and that thrill makes them feel alive. This is not why his heart pounds. No. This pounding is empty, more like an echo, like the remnants of a life that once was, but is no longer. Just as the auditorium darkens, Annie arrives. She flashes that broad smile and sits beside him. He takes her hand, holds it tightly. Tightly. She glances at him, puzzled, but also warmly satisfied. She loves him. He will do anything for her. Anything.

Annie. Sophie.

This is all he has left.

Chapter 14

The Vulture:

A vulture is placed in a pen 6 feet wide, 8 feet long, and at the top entirely open. In spite of this freedom, the bird will be an absolute prisoner. Here's why. When a vulture takes off from the ground, it always begins with a 10 to 12 foot running start. This is nothing more than the bird's habit. Without space to run, the vulture will not even attempt flight, but will, for the rest of its life, be a prisoner, trapped in a small jail with no top...

KELLY HYDEN CLOSES HER EYES and rests her head against the leather chair back. She doesn't read any further. She doesn't need to. The e-mail is from an aunt in Utah, who every few days forwards "inspiring" stories. Kelly rarely finds the stories inspiring and today is no exception. "What if the vulture's way is not mere habit?" she thinks. "What if the bird is designed such that, without the 12 foot runway, flight is impossible? If so, the open pen is just a cruel joke, a tease that dares hope, but delivers futility."

Six years Kelly and Pete Hyden have been married, six and a half of which have been unhappy. She isn't sure why she didn't see this coming. Maybe it was youth's innocence or maybe Pete's public charm, which during courtship was lavished upon her and didn't turn off until after the engagement was announced and after the wedding plans were in such full swing that backing out was nearly unthinkable...

...or maybe she didn't want to see it coming. Maybe she wanted to believe that the sweet, caring, witty man with whom she fell in love was not the pig she married and that someday that man would return. She leans back and studies the ceiling. Is it hope or futility? She used to dream. She used to wonder if such things were possible, but not anymore.

Kelly shuts down her computer. The screen goes dark, leaving behind a dull imprint, bare shoulders and a low cut workout top. She is curious, tilts the panel so that a shadow she recognizes as her face fills the void. Her lips are supple, her cheeks high, her hair pulled back and braided. It is a mask of happiness and plenty which conceals an existence so Spartan that should anyone chance to peek beneath it, they would not recognize this life as Kelly's. She makes the mask smile, checks it for flaws, sees none. Its perfection is both satisfying and disheartening, for she knows it is so well kept that never will these covered truths see the light of day. This knowledge creates within her a gnawing loneliness. Lightly, she runs an index finger over it: the cheek, the nose, the upper lip. Is it real? She isn't sure. The smile leaves. Light from the lamp reflects off the granite desk top and soaks into the mask, leaving everything behind it invisible. It is as if the door to the hallway, the bookcase, the paintings on the wall do not exist. There is nothing but the mask.

Inside a plastic skin, her cell phone vibrates.

"Yes?"

"Mrs. Hyden? This is Joe Johnson."

"Yes."

"Your husband asked me to call. I'd like to drop off preliminary plans and leave some samples."

"I'm home now."

"And I'm in town today. 15 minutes, ok?"

"Sure."

She lays the skin back on the desk, looks around, decides to do a quick pick up.

Adding onto the house is so unlike Pete. He is a man who cares for only two things, money and titles. Thus she suspects that, in some way, this reno service is at least one of the two.

Money. When they were kids, Frank gave each of his boys a five dollar bill. Before week's end Tom's five was spent. He bought a baseball, his contribution to the neighborhood pickup games, and two cheeseburgers, so that he and Puck could have a "business lunch".

Pete's five went into his wallet and to this day is still there. It has become a conversation piece which Pete pulls out whenever he needs to impress a potential client.

Kelly is convinced that he'll be buried with the damned thing, which probably isn't far from the truth.

Titles. In addition to his position as bank president, Pete has been president of Rotary, church council, and the hospital advisory committee. He is a past chair of the Association of Iowa Banking Professionals and just finished his second term as a Lake Pulaski School Board member where in the construction of a new high school, he was a key player. Along with Kelly, he has hosted the annual United Way drive and the last three Breast Cancer Valentine Galas.

Money and titles. Pete collects them because they serve him so well. Kelly has even come to believe that the only reason she is here, living in his house, is to satisfy his need for the titles "husband" and "father". Publically these are positions to which he is most attentive, pedaling the fiction that he is a devoted family man. As for being a real husband, a real father, Pete has lost all interest, if indeed he ever had any. For all practical purposes, Kelly and the twins are just another set of wall plaques, just three more props that service his ambitious pursuits.

To this end, Kelly does her job, plays her assigned part. Her mask is attractive, light hearted, and creates the illusion that when it comes to the Hyden enterprise, she is a full partner. She raises the children, maintains a trim figure, collects titles that compliment her husband's, and keeps her mountain of dolefulness under cover. This world of hers is, of course, a sham, and although she has never breathed a word of it Kelly hates her life, every bit of it. She hates how she has everything, but is nothing. She hates the social circles her "position" demands and all the friends that are not. She hates how full her empty world appears. She hates the way Pete treats her, the way she is expected to become invisible. The dinner parties, the social events, the fund raisers, he puts her on his arm only to toss her aside when the time comes and she is sent to work her assigned portions of the room. But most of all, she hates the way these evenings end, the drive home, the duplicity.

Take, for instance, last night. No sooner was the car door shut, than Pete began the pretense. He took her into his confidence, bashing Lora Gangstad's excessive and uncontrolled "appetite for champagne." He fed Kelly the boorish details, leaning toward her and lowering his voice as though he was passing state secrets and she was the only person in the world he could possibly trust. He winked at her. He raised his eyebrows. He cut Lora to shreds.

Kelly has come to understand that this is, in fact, not a conversation and not the conferring of his good faith. This is a rehearsal. This is Pete practicing the exact words he will use when, in a few hours, he and his golf buddies will stand on the second tee, light their stogies, and begin the verbal surgery.

Last night galled her, just as it always does. Still she played along and waited for part two, when without warning the mock trust was pulled and he cuffed her like she was some dog that failed in her performance of a stupid pet trick. "Why can't you just *sit*, Kelly. *Stay*. *Fetch* a glass of wine. *Heel* while I casually work my way across the room and introduce myself to so and so. *Play Dead* for the circle of top bank customers..."

Play dead. This one she gets right every time and she resents it. She resents him and she hates herself for how easily she takes his crap.

Kelly finishes shining the counter top, puts the last plate in the dishwasher, and surveys the finished kitchen. Everything is perfect. The doorbell rings. She glances at the mirror, checks the mask, smiles, opens the door. "Joe! Come in. Come in."

"Thank you, Mrs. Hyden."

"Please, it's Kelly."

"Yes ma'am."

She's heard about Joe. She's heard that he is both an excellent craftsman and short on social graces. Pete calls him a cold fish and wonders "why the hell Tom wastes so much time maintaining their 'do nothing' friendship." Kelly leads Joe to the kitchen table, where he spreads papers and samples. She is prepared to carry the conversation and not unexpectedly finds that small talk with Joe is like hitting tennis balls against a mattress.

Small talk: The art of filling the air with countless nothings, with aimless, purposeless, directionless words. Small talk is many things, a dance of strangers, friendship kept distant, a way of being close without being close.

For all her adult life, this is the small talk that Kelly has known and it bores her silly. Even at that, she can imagine a different kind of small talk, how thousands of little nothings could knit themselves together and become a big something; how they could form a trusting cradle in which two people might hazard a deeper intimacy. Kelly, for instance, is fascinated with Tom and Annie and the way, at family gatherings, they sit beside each other, smile in each other's ears and trade their endless stream of nothings. She imagines those conversations and the invisible hammock they knot, one strand wrapped over the next, over the next, over the next. She imagines the strength, the trusting embrace they create. She pictures the strands stretching, tightening as the weight of deeper things is safely slung into its webbing. It makes her envious.

This, of course, is small talk as she can only imagine. With the people in her life, and especially with her husband, small talk is a strategy of pretense and has, but one purpose, deflecting intimacy. Oh yes, it invites trust, it promises more, but it never, ever intends to deliver.

Joe unrolls three drawings and sets out samples, cabinet colors, base board styles, color swatches. He points to a wall, describes the new room and where it will be situated. His words are few and when he does speak the cadence is halting, almost broken. Kelly listens and understands the why of Joe's awkward reputation, but to her surprise decides that all these reports are a complete misread. She clearly sees in him something that is not at all gawky. It is more like a shyness, a tenderness, maybe even a sadness. He glances down at the drawings, which she takes as an opportunity. She studies his eyes. She spots something hauntingly familiar.

She doesn't know exactly why she changes the subject or why she asks the question. It just seems right. "So how are you doing, Joe, you know, after the baby?"

The question stops Joe. He looks at her. The look is not a stare and not a gaze. It is a searching, as though he is looking through her, or maybe in her, to find something he thinks he sees, but cannot just yet locate. Finally he catches himself, looks down, apologizes.

"I'm sorry Mrs. Hyden. It's just that...it's umm...it's been a year and a half since I've heard that question...and uh...the last person who asked didn't really want an answer."

Joe pauses, looks at the wall. "I guess the topic makes people uncomfortable. Either that or else they figure that enough time's past and everything's back to normal..."

Silence. His eyes find hers. "There is no normal. Suspect there never will be..."

Across from each other they sit, looking, but not looking at the rings and the samples they hold. Finally Joe nearly whispers, "I think you've got what you need here, ma'am. I best be on my way."

Kelly walks him to the door. He stops, looks down, then up, directly into her eyes. "Don't know why I said those things...I don't usually...it's just so...so uhh..."

"...so hard to talk about?" Kelly interrupted.

"...so risky."

Kelly glances down, absorbing what he has just said. She looks up to again meet those eyes and their continued search.

"There's no risk here, Joe."

"Yes ma'am. I...I think I know that."

Joe walks down to the driveway and his pickup. From the open door, Kelly watches.

"It's Kelly," she says.

"Yes ma'am."

He doesn't look back...

Kelly wonders how long it has been since anyone has been that genuine with her, since anyone has honored her with a piece of their own tender, vulnerable reality. It feels good. It feels like a friendship, or at least how she thinks a friendship might feel. Whatever it is, Kelly finds that something deeply human, something intensely personal, something long encapsulated within a plastic skin is vibrating, is looking up, is daring thoughts that soar.

Chapter 15

"Is it a 3 and a 1, or a 1 and a 3?"

IT HAS BEEN ONLY A few days, but already Tom wonders why this once large question has become small, so small that it is nearly irrelevant. He knows it should trouble him. He knows that the difference between the two should create a space of ambiguity, a place where restless conflict claims his soul. It used to, but now oddly it doesn't. Late last week when he crossed that threshold, the world he entered was very different from the world he expected. He expected billowing clouds. He expected to lose all sense of right, left, up, down, and when that didn't happen, it surprised the hell out of him. Quite to the contrary, crossing that threshold brought an unanticipated clarity. In it, the chalky grays that were always his traveling companion completely disappeared. They did not dissolve and create a fog. They did not dissipate and form a haze. *They disappeared.* Never has the world been this uncomplicated and Tom finds that with each passing day his new home becomes more comfortable. That which once produced a mountain of angst has been reassigned and humbled. It is now just a mind puzzle, one of life's little curiosities.

"Is it a 3 and a 1 or a 1 and a 3?

Does it really matter?"

At this moment, the only thing that does matter is last week's near screw up and how, in the future, he will avoid them. It is on these issues that Tom focuses all his energies.

He replays the incident. Tom understands that the other day when Mary interrupted, his mistakes were nearly fatal. That cannot happen again. Clearly the plan has holes and those holes must be filled. Tom starts over. He logs on and inserts a jump drive. Nothing will be saved to the computer's hard drive. There will be no server traces. Every one of Tom's secrets, those under the roll top and the Bank of Tom spreadsheets will be encrypted, password protected, and stored only here, on the jump drive. Whenever he leaves his desk, even if it is only a bathroom break, the computer's cache will be deleted and the jump drive goes with him. There will be no exceptions.

He opens a word processing document and takes notes.

Bank of Tom Rules:

1. *Everyone always gets paid.*
2. *The Bank of Tom will not be used to increase lifestyle. There will be no boats, no sports cars, no Cozumel vacation homes (maybe!). The bank has only one purpose–pay down the debt and save the family. Anything more creates an unnecessary risk.*
3. *Exit strategy: This is borrowed money, an operating loan. Once the mission is accomplished and the debt gone, limits will be set. Household spending will be slashed. The Hydens*

will live within their means. Between these limits and an income no longer dedicated to meeting minimums, the operating loan—every single penny of it—will be repaid. Once the money is returned, The Bank of Tom closes its doors. Everything will be as it was.
4. Simplicity is a virtue.
    a. To all "income sources", Bank of Tom "loans" must remain unnoticeable.
    b. To the auditors, Bank of Tom deposits must look like everyday business.
    c. Nothing happens without a well-considered procedure. All procedures will be regularly evaluated. All procedures will be followed to the letter! Again there will be no exceptions.

Flow Chart:
How funds become available.

Tom stops, thinks about this portion of the flow chart and how it is already well established. He also recognizes that a solid plan is not enough. Stealing is as much art as it is science. It is knowing people, who they are, how they work. It is knowing habits, time of day. It is understanding that everyone and everything, himself included, are pieces of a whole, woven threads that form a single blanket. This is the given tapestry and within its fabric, he must work. He will not, for instance, borrow from Wesley Flooring. Jeri, the Wesley bookkeeper, runs a tight department. He will, on the other hand, borrow from Jensen Farms, Hunter's Tiling and Drainage, Goodman's Plumbing, businesses where either the bookkeeping is loose or the staff is small and day to day operations are such that eyeing every statement and tracking every item is an impossibility. These loan accounts will become Bank of Tom income sources.

Next Tom thinks about his auditors. He knows how they do their work, what does and does not receive their scrutiny. A picture of Lakeland Savings and Trust emerges. It looks like a folded blanket, some surfaces are plainly visible while others provide opportunity, places where he can safely cloak his activities.

He begins typing.

1. Appropriate Lakeland Savings and Trust (LST) customers are identified and their accounts tracked. When one of these customers makes a large loan payment that payment is recorded incorrectly.
2. The incorrect entry creates, on one side, a surplus (which will become The Bank of Tom funds) and, on the other, a short fall (to the LST customer account).
3. A couple of days later, another large loan payment will be recorded incorrectly and a portion of this "error" will cover the above mentioned short fall.

How money is moved from LST to the Bank of Tom.

Tom pauses, remembers. Last week he had the right idea, but loose procedures nearly sunk him. The movement of this money must be well disguised. It must look like regular bank business. He thinks about how the bank spends money, about the office supply houses, furniture stores, janitorial services, abstract companies, and law firms that sell LST their goods and services. These vendors bill Lakeland and when payment is tendered send receipts.

Tom continues.

1. Open several new bank accounts (with other banks). Each account will be associated with a current LST vendor.

Vendor	Bank of Tom Account
Office Buddy	North American Trust
Zeta's Business Equipment	Great Northern Bank of Iowa
Iowa Abstract	Bank of the Mid-West (Act 6737842)
Mid-Iowa Janitorial	Bank of the Mid-West (Act 5420221)
Harvey and Sons	Sandy Savings and Trust
Midwest Security Systems	Citizens Bank of Lake Pulaski

Because these businesses are already established Lakeland vendors, they will become the Bank of Tom laundry mechanism. Using old invoices and receipts, Tom will create blanks, the canvasses on which he will produce legitimate looking paper work.

2. Develop both an electronic trail and a paper trail.
   a. Generate invoices from LST vendors.
   b. Enter these payments into LST's books.
   c. Generate vendor receipts.
   d. File invoices and receipts.
3. Deposit these payments (either electronically or by check) in the corresponding Bank of Tom account.

Tom saves the file, leans back, thinks how, in real life, this will work. "Last Tuesday the Bucholtz transaction yielded $720. Today it will be Jensen Farms. I will transpose a 1 and a 3 for a 3 and a 1, yielding an $1800 surplus. Of this 1800, $720 pays Bucholtz and the rest, $1080, will be recorded as 3 payments, Harvey and Sons, Midwest Security, and Iowa Abstract. Lakeland's books will show all the proper entries. Corresponding invoices and receipts will be generated and properly filed. These payments will be deposited in the Bank of Tom laundry accounts. Then...I pay my bills."

Tom doesn't know it yet, but his new bank's success will surprise him. By the end of the month, all his minimums will be satisfied and the mortgage payment made. By the next month Tom will pay down 3 credit cards. After six months, all debt will be erased and he will be handling a cash surplus. He doesn't know this yet. Right now, he sees only two things.

He sees Jensen's check and how easily a 3 becomes a 1 and a 1 becomes a 3.

He sees Annie and Sophie. It occurs to him that their wellbeing is the source of this newfound limpidity. A couple of days ago, he was afraid that he might lose his way, but now that he has crossed the threshold, everything is new and clear. It is, to be sure, a dark clarity, but the purpose is unquestionable and it creates its own right, its own wrong, and its own sense of direction. Right, left, up, down, it is all there. He glances down and sees the safety line. From his dive reel, a thin, white string extends toward an exit that no longer exists. Oddly this does not cause him panic. Everything else, Annie, Sophie, the plan, the bank and its operation, everything is vivid and so right. That the safety line disappears into nothing, that the Bank of Tom has erased the exit, these things do not concern him. Slow his breathing? Check his gauges? He feels no need. He even wonders why he waited so long. Why did he not take these measures years ago? There is a calm and it is so unearthly that it must emanate from a place beyond nature. He knows that tonight he will sleep, and will do so without movies, mad dogs, or balance beams. He will slumber. In water dark yet clear, he will slumber.

How can this be? He does not know. For now, he hopes that this place is as real as it seems. He hopes that the crystal clarity is not some cruel ruse. He considers the impossibility of it all and he hopes. He hopes that it is not.

Chapter 16

A SMALL RED LIGHT BLINKS, turns green. The telephone speaks. "Mr. Hyden, your 10:30 has arrived."

"Thank you, Lindsay. I'll be out shortly."

A single light shines, a bright circle forms. Against his cherry desktop the light reflects and scatters, casting dim shadows around an otherwise dark room. When alone, Pete pulls the shades and beneath this single light sets his work. He likes it this way. This bright circle brings focus, clarity. Everything else, with its subtleties, its lesser lights, its endless shades of gray recedes, nearly disappears. Here black is black and white is white. Here yes and no are just that, nothing less and nothing more. Here he can see things, or rather that one thing as it is. The universe becomes the light and its object. So when, for instance Pete must fire an employee, the situation is placed beneath the light and all surrounding ambiguities, the family needing a paycheck, the lives that will be changed all disappear. The light and whatever Pete sets beneath it, this is the entire universe.

This morning Pete examines three papers, checks the numbers, slides them inside a manila folder, and sets aside the folder. With this task completed, he reaches behind his chair and louvers the blinds. Diffused sunlight sifts through the openings and the room blossoms. Soft shadows and interesting subtleties fold around the desk, credenza, and bookcases. The entire room appears and Pete fills it. On slate colored walls, his many accolades are now visible; service club recognitions, achievement awards, athletic honors, photos of Kelly and the boys. Each carefully chosen piece builds a visual resume, Pete the philanthropist, Pete the citizen, Pete the athlete, Pete the family man. Taken together, an image of prominence and success emerges.

It is, of course, just that, an image. In truth, Pete is a man of layers, two of which are visible. There is the Pete that "everyone is supposed to see" and there is the Pete that a "few too many" know.

So...

Pete appears calm.

    He is stretched tighter than a violin string.

Pete looks gracious.

    He keeps score.

        Be it golf, community service recognitions,

            or tracking business competitors,

                with everything Pete keeps score.

    He holds grudges.

    He remembers.

Pete projects peacefulness, patience.

    He is a smoldering volcano

        where under his calm surface anger builds,

            impatience boils.

Pete appears easy going, adaptable.
>   He is shrewd, political,
>   > and skillfully uses his easy exterior
>   >   > as a maneuvering tool.

Pete seems kind.
>   He is a bitter man,
>   > driven by anger
>   >   > and obsessed with his ambitious pursuits.

Some would call this duplicity, phoniness, but the matter is not that simple. It never is, not with Pete, not with anyone. There are, in fact, things about a person's life that make that person what they are, and if everyone could just see those constitutional elements, the rest would make perfect sense. Of course, these are also the kinds of things that, for one reason or another, folks keep hidden. So it is with Pete. Pete's public persona, that which "everyone is supposed to see", is one of graciousness, charm, wit, altruism. While it is true that if he could be whatever he wanted to be, this is what Pete would choose for himself, he cannot make such choices. They are beyond his reach. There are in fact unseen and irresistible forces locking him into trajectories he cannot change. From multiple directions they pull and tug, warp and distort what he wants to be and shape him into what he is. Thus there is the second Pete, the man beneath the man, the man who is calculating, spiteful, hard driving, ambitious, untrustworthy. Try as he may, these things Pete cannot change.

Of course, the "few too many" who see the man beneath the man believe that this is the real Peter Hyden. His competitors, his golf buddies, the folks in his social circles, his brother, even Kelly, they all think they know Pete. They believe that they've got a bead on who he is, what makes him tick, and why he can't be trusted, but they don't, not really. They see only the second layer, only bitterness, only resentment. They know only the effects, but not the causes. What they cannot see are the layers beneath the layers; fundamental forces that continually press and mold him into this twisted shape. They cannot see Pete's youth, his father's firm hand and the expectations that came with Frank's demanding guidance. They cannot feel the terrible disparity, how Pete was held to an unyielding standard, how he was saddled with the task of carrying the family name while his older brother was set free. Tom rode bikes, played ball, spent his nights lying in the grass and mindlessly watching the stars and the billions of miles between them. All the while Pete was resume building. He became the student body president, he brought home every single academic honor, and the only lights under which he would find himself were those of Friday night. Those lights shined like the one on his desk, focusing attention upon a single spot, making everything beneath the lights large and everything outside the lights small, insignificant. Yes, those lights shone, and with them the helmet, the pads, the ball, the cheering crowds, and the 100 yards of glory, where he, Peter Franklin Hyden was the firmament's brightest star.

At the time, Pete did not understand that Frank had already given up on Tom. At the time, Pete did not know that behind the judging eye and in those unbending requirements was a father's love. All he felt were the single-minded demands. All he knew were the relentless expectations that hammered him, shaped him, and eventually formed him into the hardened thing that he has now become. Of course, this upbringing engineered to shape and form Pete also pushed him to the very edge, until his father's wrath became his wrath, and his father's anger became his anger, and his father's drivenness became his ardor, his ruthlessness, his ambition.

So bitterness ferments, becomes anger. So resentment sours the soul, spawns hatred. Publicly Pete admires his father. Secretly he despises him. Publicly Pete embraces Tom. Secretly he resents him and is embarrassed by Tom's many public failures.

Duplicity? Phoniness? The matter is never that simple. The opposing strands of graciousness and visceral bitterness, kindness and instinctive resentment are completely and hopelessly intertwined, and while it does not excuse what Pete has become, it does explain.

Pete sets the folder on the side of his otherwise clean desk, louvers the blinds, and waits. This is by design. In a couple of minutes, he will bring Johnson into his office and they will talk business, discuss the new addition, review the three bids. Pete, of course, already knows the outcome. Joe will do the work. When the work is finished, he wants to stand behind his new bar, pour potential clients drinks, and crow. "Look at the workmanship. I hired Johnson, got the best..." So while Pete has already decided who will do the job, he is not about to tell Joe. No. He makes Joe wait. He lets Joe think, maybe even sweat. Even before Joe walks through the door, the games have begun.

Pete walks toward the door. "Joe or Puck?" he wonders to himself and then quickly decides that "Puck sounds phony, like I'm chumming with a guy I don't know."

"Jooe." Pete lengthens the 'o' and extends his hand. "Thank you. Thank you for taking time. I know how busy you must be. Please come in."

In truth, Pete has heard that lately Joe's business has been slow, a fact that figures into his strategy.

"Thank you, Mr. Hyden."

Pete's handshake is firm, but not too firm; it conveys confidence.

He looks Joe straight in the eye and holds the pose a bit longer than Joe expects. This is a ploy designed to make Joe uncomfortable, and it appears to work. Joe looks away. Pete sees this.

"You know Joe," Pete smiles warmly, "you call me Mr. Hyden and I'm looking over my shoulder, checking for the old man... Please, it's Pete."

"Yes sir."

"How are things with you, Joe? It's Jen, right?"

Joe's answers are short, uncomfortable. "Yes sir. It's Jen. Things are fine."

Pete sees everything, Joe's eyes and where they look, his posture, the way Joe nervously plays with his fingers. He processes every bit of information and analyzes potential opportunities. Everything he sees confirms his initial perceptions. Joe can be had.

Pete opens the folder and lays out the three pieces of paper. "I don't normally do this, Joe. I mean a bid is a bid, right?...but I'd like to work with you on this." Pete turns the papers toward Joe and slides them across the desk. "Notice. Your bid is 12% higher than Bucholtz Contracting and 15% higher than Wertz."

Joe studies the papers and silently nods.

"Do you have an explanation?"

"You get what you pay for." To Pete, it almost sounds like Joe is asking a question.

Pete pauses, leans back, projects control. "Look Joe, you're my brother's friend. That makes you a friend of mine. I'd love to toss you the business, but you know how it goes, the numbers are the numbers."

Pete waits for a response, but gets none. This creates an uncomfortable silence, which Pete seizes. Long ago his father taught him that "the one who holds the silence holds the room" and Pete masterfully grabs every such moment. Pete, in fact, often brags that simply by leaning back and lighting a cigar, he can talk a car salesman down. He slides the papers back toward himself, pretends he's studying the numbers, waits.

"Tell you what," he pauses, "If you can match the low bid, the job is yours."

Joe's eyes are fixed on the floor. "Umm...Pete, if cost is...umm... an issue, I mean if you can't afford it...umm...then you probably don't want me." Joe gets up, extends a hand. "Thanks for letting me bid. I'm sure Wertz will do you right."

The move so surprises Pete that he can't get up. The silence he held now holds him. Anger builds. He holds it back, recalculates, considers continuing the bluff, but quickly decides otherwise. This recovery takes only a second and is so seamless that Joe cannot possibly read Pete's retreat. Pete leans back, smiles wryly, and in a gesture of visible surrender, shakes his head. "Have a seat Joe." He opens his desk drawer, finds a pen and his checkbook.

The other two bids are crumpled and tossed in the wastebasket. Pete signs the contract, writes a check.

"When can you start?"

Pete has underestimated Joe. He hates losing.

It won't happen again.

Chapter 17

Tom comes home. The television is dark, the radio off. It is so quiet, that had Annie's car not been in the garage, he would have guessed that no one is home. Then from the kitchen Tom hears a sound. It is the rapid, intense scraping of a spatula against a plate. The refrigerator door opens, then closes. There is more scraping. Taken together the noises have an anxious quality. Tom sighs, enters the kitchen. Annie is waiting. On the granite counter top a stack of papers sit, Sophie's math worksheets.

He kisses Annie's cheek. "How's it going honey?" He already knows the answer.

"Tom, take a look at this." Annie's spatula becomes a pointer. "C pluses," Annie's tone is a mix of distress and incredulity, "all five of them. C pluses!! I wouldn't care, except I know she's a better student than this. She is not hitting her potential."

Tom doesn't smile. He holds the papers, intently examines

~ Rapture of the Deep ~

them, shakes his head. He tries projecting a troubled image, Annie needs to see that he is as concerned as is she.

"Did you talk with her?"

"Yes, yes. Her parent teacher conference was this afternoon. The teacher was wonderful. She told me that Sophie is a lovely girl. I'm proud of her, you know that Tom, but she can do better than this. I know she can. On the way home, we talked, but I'm sure it didn't do any good."

"We talked..." Tom knows what this means. Too many times he has watched these unpleasant episodes. Annie lectures while Sophie hangs her head and makes herself small.

There is a long silence which Tom knows he is supposed to fill. He is supposed to support Annie, take her side. He's supposed to step up, reinforce both her hard line and the train wreck it produced. "You know how it is, honey. Sophie always struggles with math." The comment seeks a softer middle ground. He knows it won't succeed. He tries anyway.

"Sure," Annie not only misses the opening, but Tom's attempt clearly irritates her, "and that's exactly why we're hiring a tutor, that's why I help her with this stuff. She can do better, Tom, and it's our job to see to it. Just this morning Dr. Lisa was talking about this. 'Love is action. Action is love.' We've got to do something here. We can't just let it be. If we don't act, she'll never 'reach her untapped potential'. It will be like—like we don't care."

Dr. Lisa. Her pop psychology, her feel good, guilt heaping crap turns Tom's stomach. Then there is the "like we don't care" comment, Annie's little litmus test. He wants to object, but fights back the urge, holds his tongue and does what he always does. He patronizes Annie. It is not a mocking patronization. It is a loving condescension, more like holding her hand, like walking her through what she perceives as an impossible situation, an impasse. Today he is especially attentive. Annie is visibly upset, more so than usual. Minimizing the issue or pursuing compromise will only make things worse. It will be ruled as "Tom selling out." Right now Annie needs both his steady resolve and his calm.

"Where is she?" His voice is hopeful and hides his sense of resignation.

"In her room."

"Let me go talk to her."

Tom gives Annie a hug. Annie halfheartedly reciprocates. "Don't worry about it, honey." he reassures her, "We'll get it fixed. The three of us, we'll work on it together."

"I just want her to be the best she can be."

"I know that sweetheart. I love you."

"I love you, too."

Sophie's door is shut and Tom knows exactly what this means. So when he knocks and peeks inside, there are no surprises. Sophie is lying on her bed, her tender figure wrapped around her pillow. Her cheeks are wet, her eyes red, her nose runny. She sniffs and her entire body involuntarily recoils.

"Hey pumpkin'."

"Hi daddy."

Tom sits on the edge of her bed and lays a hand across Sophie's shoulder. Gently he rubs her back.

"Sooo, I heard you had conferences today."

"Yeah."

"How did it go? Tell me about it, pea."

"Mommy's not very happy with me. I'm not very good."

This triggers something. Gently Tom pushes her shoulder and rolls Sophie over. The two of them are now face to face. "Listen to me, Soph, this is important. It's more important than gymnastics, more important than school, or math, or grades or anything."

Sophie is drawn into his eyes. They are brown, deep, and more kind than anything she has ever known. In her little world, sometimes her daddy's eyes are the only thing that makes sense. Today, however, his kindness is mixed with an urgency and for the moment makes her forget her sadness.

"Don't you ever say that you're not very good." Tom's tone is direct, earnest. "It's not true. Don't you know, Sophie, you are the most amazing thing in the universe."

"Daaddy..." Sophie smiles her protests, but Tom gently puts his index finger over her lip. It stops her.

"No. I mean it Soph. God made you so special...and he put you into my life, into mommy's life. You're here for a purpose, and I love you so much sweetheart. So don't you *ever* say you're not very good. You're the best thing in the world. You're certainly the best thing that ever happened to mommy and to me." Sophie's eyes are fixed upon Tom's. In his eyes, she finds ever new confidence, she always has. When everything around her brings accusations, pronounces failure, or has her believing that she's lacking, she knows that here, in her daddy's eyes she sees a singularly profound affirmation. His confidence is contagious and it lifts her. It emboldens her. With the side of his thumb, Tom wipes her cheek. He smiles at her. She smiles back.

"Now listen, I want you to do something. When you get to thinking you're not very good, I want you to get to the nearest mirror, look into your own eyes, and say 'Sophie...'"

Sophie's sneaky smile is so genuine that it makes Tom pause. He quickly recovers. "...Sophie old girl, they're lying to you again. Don't believe 'um, darling. Don't believe 'um."

Tom pauses, smiles. "OK, your turn. Go ahead and say it."

Sophie giggles, blushes. "That's corny..."

Tom raises his eyebrows, cocks his head. "Hey. This is important."

They say it together. "Sophie old girl, they're lying to you again. Don't believe 'um, darling. Don't believe 'um."

This time they both giggle. Then Tom again becomes earnest. "You know your mamma. She just wants the best for you. That's because she loves you, Soph. Just do your best, always do your very best and always remember that you are the most special thing in the universe. Do that and you can't ever go wrong."

"I love you, daddy."

"I love you too, pumpkin'...So, you hungry?"

"Yeah."

"Remember what I said now. OK?"

"Yeah."

"Good! Now, hop on, and after supper we'll do math together." Tom presents his back and Sophie climbs aboard. The ride becomes a gallop that takes them through the hallway and into the kitchen. They're both giggling. This makes Annie so happy. Knowing that Tom has smoothed things over brightens her.

Later that evening, Tom wants to say something. There is so much that Annie should know. She should better understand Sophie and what motivates her. She should see that it's affirmation and not challenge that builds Sophie's confidence, drives her, and brings her success. He wishes Annie could consider a different approach. He wants to say something, but decides against it. He doesn't know why. Maybe he doesn't want another tangle. Maybe he knows she'd be offended. What he does know is that he is the family buffer, a role that for both of them is vital. Thus he reaches in both directions, softens Annie's hard edges, builds Sophie up. It is a good job, a noble job, and when he's successful, nothing gives him more satisfaction. Still he wishes it could be different. He wishes that on their own, they could find each other. He wishes...

Chapter 18

THE RADIO IS OFF. HE used to listen, but not anymore. Now windshield time is open space, no music, no news, no stupid call-in shows. It's just open space, poignant and pointless, quiet and noisy, peaceful and anxious. His truck hums. The transmission winds up and ratchets down. Joe drives. This space with its hard everything and death-like nothing, is a reflection of his life and in it he finds himself fighting an impulse. Push the button, crank up the volume, saturate his senses. Let the radio do what it does so well, provide a mindless escape.

Today, as with most days, he imagines Jen sitting beside him. He sees the two of them talking, fighting, giving a shit. It makes him smile. It makes him hurt. He wishes it could be.

He pictures her sadness, her aching heart, her spirit drenched in whiskey. It makes him want her all the more and he cannot understand why the gravity their hardships naturally create have not done their job, have not drawn them together. It always had. Why won't it now?

He drives. On this particular morning, he is opening a new job site, Pete Hyden's man-cave. The lane on which the Hydens live is strikingly beautiful. Ash trees form a lush, green tunnel. Over and above him, their branches spread and canopy the street. Of course, Joe doesn't notice this. Instead he sees what others cannot. He looks inside the trees, beneath the bark. He sees spirals, lines, knots and how they could become tables, chairs, cabinets, handmade veneers. He imagines where, inside the trunks, each table leg, each chair back, each cabinet door is positioned. He sees the tree's lesser portion, that which is unfit for crafting fine furniture. He knows this wooded tunnel not only for what it now is, but for its embedded potential and how when one life is finished another might emerge. There is so much that Joe sees, so much hidden from everyone else.

A long time ago, he saw his wife and who she was. He saw depth, richness, challenge, a raw beauty revealed only to him. Lovingly peeling away her many delicate layers, carefully exposing her richly contoured spirit, this had always been life's unquestioned purpose, but now? Now, Joe's not sure. Is there anything left? He's doesn't know. He wonders if maybe this tree called their marriage has completely rotted, if maybe all that remains is a fragile exterior, a shell that looks healthy, but will soon collapse. He drives. Open space surrounds him. He wonders how he can save her, if he can save her.

He pulls into the Hyden driveway. Until this moment, he has not thought about Kelly or their first conversation. There, in the driveway, he remembers the exchange and it warms him.

Before he can ring the bell, the door swings open.

"Hi!" A boy's squeaky voice draws Joe's eyes downward.

"What's your name, buddy?"

"Franklin. They call me Frankie."

"Got it. OK Frankie, in the back of my truck there's a tool belt. Wanna get it for me?"

"Sure!" Down the sidewalk, Frankie dashes.

Into the doorway, another boy appears. He looks *exactly* like the first. "I'm Petie. Can I help, too?"

"You bet. Black case, right next to the tool belt."

"Oookaay. !" Petie is right behind his brother.

"Well, you're quite the charmer." Joe looks up and sees Kelly who is standing on the steps. She has a book tucked beneath her arm and is carrying a coffee cup. "Good to see you, Joe."

"Yes ma'am."

Up the walk, the twins clamor, their loads a bit more than they can carry.

"Boys! Be careful!!" Kelly's warning is urgent, but warmly soft.

"It's OK." Joe smiles, "Tools are made for abuse. Put 'um over there, guys."

Kelly rounds up the boys and takes them to school. By the time she returns Joe's workspace is set and the job has begun.

Kelly putzes around the kitchen and every so often eyes the progress. Even as he demolishes a wall, Joe is meticulous, measured, careful. Kelly acts as though she's busy, brews more coffee, makes a grocery list, chops carrots. She watches. A half an hour passes and from the kitchen she emerges, bringing a coffee pot and two mugs.

"Wanna cup?"

Without looking up, Joe replies. "Yes ma'am." Kelly lays her hand over his forearm. The hand is light, soft, and it stops his work. It draws his eyes into her own.

"Kelly?" She reminds him.

"Kelly." He nods his head slightly.

They stand and in silence sip coffee. Usually, such dead space makes Kelly nervous, but not here, not with Joe. Over her cup and its rising steam, she watches him. He is completely comfortable. Never has she met someone for whom silence is such a native environment and breaking the moment almost pains her, but she has to ask.

"Sooo...what happened yesterday, between you and Pete?"

"What do you mean?"

"Well, when he came home last night he was in a serious pout. I asked about the reno and who he hired. He lowered his head, said 'Johnson', plopped himself on the couch, and started killing channels." As Kelly tells the story she mimics Pete's demeanor. Her imitation is so perfect, Joe can't hide the smile. "You must'a busted him up."

"Not that I saw." Joe replies, "Your husband wanted me to lower my bid. When I told him I couldn't, he hired me anyway."

"Well, I'm impressed. Not many people get the best of Peter Hyden."

She lifts the pot. Joe holds out his cup and takes the refill.

The exchange creates a lull, which Kelly instinctively wants to fill. She resists and the empty moment blossoms, becomes full, becomes rich with contentment, or is it expectation? She isn't sure. All she knows is that this is *not* how she experiences others. With others, moments like this are awkward, anxious, demanding small talk. Of course such filling stunts fullness, a fact that until now she'd never recognized. The emptiness and its richness surprise her and Kelly wishes it would last. She looks into Joe's eyes and again sees a sadness. She lets go and soon the conversation leads itself.

This time it's Joe who first speaks. "I want to...to thank you for our last conversation."

"How are you doing?"

"Honestly?" He looks at Kelly.

She raises her eyebrows as if to say, "It's OK."

"Not good," he finishes. "I miss my wife. I want her back"

"What do you mean?"

"After Joey, we've...I don't know...she's been gone. There's nothing there and it hurts. It's like...like a phantom pain."

"Phantom pain?" Kelly stops him. "What...what do you mean?"

Joe pauses. Thinks. "When a limb has been severed...you know...an arm, a hand, a foot, there is a pain where that limb used to be. If you closed your eyes, you would swear that something's still attached, that it's an open wound, hurting out to the fingertips, hurting out to the toes, just hurting. And you want someone to change the bandage. You want to take drugs, kill the pain. Only you look down and realize that the arm, the leg, it isn't there anymore. The pain is still there, but the limb is gone." Joe pauses, withdraws. Kelly waits, listens. "I wonder...I wonder sometimes if Jen and I, if we haven't become just that, a phantom pain, a remnant of something that was there, but is no longer."

"It's got to hurt, Joe," Kelly says.

"Hurts like hell...I don't know. I don't know what I'd do without her, but then I realize how long it's been since, since I've had her. She's been gone for...I don't know...seems like forever...and I find myself wondering. I've forgotten what it's like to have a wife. We don't talk. We don't touch. We don't..."

His voice tails off. He looks away. Is he crying? Kelly isn't sure.

"Jen's been drinking hard..."

Joe pauses. "Drinking hard." This is the first time these words have been spoken aloud and hearing himself say it makes the matter unbearably real.

"She sleeps all the time. She's missing a bunch of work...Tries to hide all this stuff, but she can't. I know her too well. I see it all..."

"...Kelly, it's killing me...I miss her...so much...so..."

The silence and its fullness saturate the room. They both look down. For the longest time, they look down. "I don't know why I tell you these things." Joe finishes, "I've not even told Hyd...I mean Tom..."

"...I envy you." This time it's Kelly who breaks the silence and her words pull Joe's eyes off the floor and into hers. He looks confused. He doesn't understand. He can't imagine what she means.

"What you're missing, I've never had..."

The weight sinks in. Joe nods.

Finally, he says "Best get back to work." He reaches over to return the cup. Their fingers brush. It is a soft, yet deeply physical connection and it tenderly completes the conversation.

The two of them work. Joe demolishes, cleans debris. Kelly gets groceries, exercises, prepares supper. Something is happening. Maybe it's because she is so unaccustomed to friendships, to sharing vulnerability, but something is happening and Kelly doesn't know what exactly it is. Joe, on the other hand, does and it worries him. He cuts away the walls, hauls out doors, kicks himself. With his ability to see so clearly, it is not at all clear why he didn't see this coming.

Two o'clock rolls around and Kelly again appears, this time carrying a lemonade pitcher and two tumblers. "Break time." she smiles.

"Yes. Thank you ma'am."

"Hey, what's this ma'am stuff? Kelly. Remember?"

"I'm sorry, Kelly," Joe looks down, "but there is something about this that is beginning to...to feel dangerous."

"Joe I told you that what you say to me is safe. I give you my word."

"Yes, I know and that's why it's dangerous. You're vulnerable.

I'm vulnerable. Maybe it's just me, but I know I need to keep this distance. Kelly, you need to be 'Mrs. Hyden.' You need to be 'ma'am'. You need to work on your marriage and so do I."

"Joe, I don't have friends, *any friends*. It feels so good to just...to be real with someone. I see what you're saying. I know it's a slippery slope, but if you're willing to have coffee with me, I'll be careful. We'll both be careful."

"I just don't want anyone to get hurt."

"Neither do I. I...I think we're on the same page." Kelly pauses. "So...Coffee?"

Joe smiles. "Coffee it is."

They finish their lemonade. They chat. They agree that they will be friends. They go back to work, but there is a truth here, a truth to which neither of them gives voice. The truth is this: Kelly knows there is no working on her marriage. The truth is this: Joe knows that his wife might be just a phantom pain.

School is over and Kelly brings the boys home. They are determined to 'help' Joe, so she shoos them outside. He cleans his workspace, packs his tools, heads for the door.

"Back tomorrow?"

"Oh yeah. Be here for the next several weeks."

"See you, Joe."

"Good night, Kelly."

She calls behind him, "It's Mrs. Hyden."

Joe smiles, "Yes ma'am."

Chapter 19

THE SUN HAS SET COMPLETELY. The western sky contains just a faint orange glow and stars are still but a promise. It is evening's time between, moonless and empty. For a moment, and just for a moment Joe's pit provides the only light.

Joe lets the flame diminish. Toward him the darkness creeps and he welcomes it. Soon the yellow light altogether disappears. Variegated embers glow, randomly brightening and darkening. It gives the appearance of movement, orange and black swells, like a rolling sea rising and falling. Everything outside the pit is black. Into this ocean, Joe tosses another wedge which forms a dark island. Almost immediately its grainy splinters light, char, wilt. Flames rise, splash, and finally consume the island. In its glow, Jen, Annie, Tom, Sophie stand, crouch, sit.

Once a month, sometimes more often, but at least once a month, the Hydens and Johnsons get together. Sometimes it is

Sparky's for pizza and beer. Sometimes it is Annie's back deck and a bottle of wine. Most often they meet here, the fire pit.

This particular gathering is long overdue. For several weeks, Tom and Annie have been concerned. Although neither of them know the what or why, it is clear that Puck and Jen have hit a rough patch. Annie is, of course, the perfect prescription and she knows it. When Puck called with the invite, Annie altered her plans, told her girlfriends "another night." While bonfires don't excite her like they do Tom and Sophie, tonight she is determined. She will be there, she will do her part and she wouldn't have it any other way. Tom watches Annie being Annie, her easy fun, her laughter, the way she makes conversation float and it makes him happy. Tom thinks he sees Puck and Jen trading smiles and wonders if maybe they have turned a corner, if maybe an old warmth is rekindled.

The conversation is light, lively. Tom and Joe talk about last weekend's dive. This is Annie's first opening, "Why do you two drive all the way over to Miner's when you could dive Pulaski?" Everyone laughs. You see, there is no lake anywhere near Lake Pulaski. The closest body of water is 22 miles north, just across the Minnesota border. How Lake Pulaski got its name is something of a mystery. Was there once a lake here? No one can say. One thing is certain. That name has been an endless source of fun. Just last year the City Council approved new welcome signs. They read:

Lake Pulaski
If you're looking for a lake that isn't here,
then you've come to the right place.

"What's wrong", Annie is on a roll, "Don't like the hard water?"

Tom wryly smiles. Puck offers a typical deadpan response. "I've never dove with a shovel and I'm not going to start now."

The banter lifts even Jen.

Jen and Annie couldn't be more different. They have different tastes, different likes and dislikes. They keep different social circles, but still there is a connection. Neither of them can explain it, but between them exists something more than their husband's friendship. They enjoy the other's company. They bring out the best in each other.

Sophie needs to use the bathroom. Annie and Jen walk her to the house and while there make popcorn. Puck hands Tom another beer.

Beer. Unlike whiskey and its isolationist hazards, for Puck and Tom beer is communal, almost sacramental. There is a sharing that takes place, both physical and emotional. The two of them twist their caps, stand over the fire, sip, open up, share their lives. They each hold a bottle and it brings them together. They drink together, they talk, laugh, even cry together. Tom kills the last sudsy sip. Puck hands him another and with it comes an unspoken invitation.

"So what's happening, Puck? You and Jen. You two ok?"

Joe's smile fades. "I don't know..."

Tom is matter of fact. "Listen, I know you don't want to talk about it, but I also know that if I don't pester you, this thing will stay inside until you explode. Common Puck! What's going on?"

Joe pauses. "Truth is, Hyden, it's what's *not* going on. Ever since Joey, she's, well she's shut down. You've seen it. She won't talk, she won't laugh. Hell she won't even fight. It's like there's four walls and no windows and no doors. It's like nobody's home."

"Jeeze! Joey was over two years ago."

"Yeah. I know. That's why I took her to Coz. Should have taken you guys with us, but I thought maybe if we did this alone, together...you know...that maybe she'd open up, maybe we'd...we'd reconnect."

"And???"

"Nothing. It wasn't bad, but it wasn't good either. I mean at first it looked promising. She wanted to dive, so before we left, I helped her with the book work. We got down there and she did her checkout dives, got certified, the whole thing. And the diving??? It was great! I think she liked it—don't know for sure. We went to dinner every night, walked the square. I held her hand, took her shopping. It wasn't like we fought or anything. In fact, a knock down drag out would have done a world of good. You know how she is. No, it was more like nothing, like...like she doesn't care..."

There is a long silence. "I don't know what to do, Hyden."

"Puck, you and Jen have hit the skids before, but this is different, isn't it?"

"You said it..." Joe pauses, thinks over what he's about to say. His tone darkens. "There's more, partner..."

"Hey you two," Annie's voice cuts through the night, "Solvin' the world's problems?"

Out of the black, Sophie appears first. She skips over and hugs Tom's leg. Jen and Annie follow. Annie is carrying a big popcorn bowl and talking. Jen is smiling, even giggling. The two are almost giddy which Tom takes as a positive sign. "Jen poured me up a little witches brew." Annie squints her eyes and puckers her lips, "Feels better than it tastes!"

Tom sees Puck lower his head, reach for a log, feed the fire. He wonders...

"No, we're just reliving Eldo." Tom refers to the pond as if it is an old friend. "Speaking of which, what did you think of diving Jen?"

"It was amazing." Jen smiles the words, "Absolutely amazing." She takes a sip, checks the bottom of her cup, then turns to Sophie. "Did Joe tell you about the eagle ray? It's a kind of like great big sting ray, Sophie. It had spots, and wings...like this." Jen flaps her arms. "Looked like it was flying through the water."

"Wooow... Really???"

"Yeah. I mean, I get it now. I never understood why your dad is so dive crazy, but now? I can't wait to go back. You know Annie, you need to give it a try."

"Ok, did my husband put you up to this?" Annie teases, takes another sip, "You know, he talks about diving like it's some kind of religion."

Annie's voice contains a tension that only Tom hears. He knows the source.

Several years ago, Annie did try diving. It wasn't that she necessarily wanted to. The idea had, in fact, always made her nervous, but she knew how much Tom loved it. So she shelved her anxiety hoping to make diving something they could share. An hour with an instructor and she was ready for the pool. Over and over again the instructor told her that "this is different than swimming. When you swim, you hold your breath, right? When you dive, you never ever hold your breath. Always you breathe." Annie smiled, nodded. They geared up and stood in the shallow end. Annie bent over, put her face in the water, drew a breath, blew bubbles. Everything worked perfectly. Then came the next step, diving the deep end and with it a sensation for which Annie was completely unprepared. She let the air out of her vest and began her descent. As the water covered her, she did what came naturally, she held her breath, and held her breath, and held her breath. Clamped between her teeth was all the air she'd ever need, but Annie panicked! She spit the regulator out of her mouth and frantically swam to the surface, but because she was weighted to sink, she couldn't fight nature's forces. Of course, the instructor knew exactly what was happening. Annie was never in any real danger. It made no difference. Annie vowed to never again venture beneath the surface. Tom has never again mentioned it.

"...he talks about diving like it's some kind of religion."

Tom doesn't find her eyes. It isn't necessary. He hears the fear he cannot fix. Annie needs the surface. She needs shallow water, where beneath her feet she can feel the pool bottom. Breathing topside air, this is what she needs, and when she cannot, when, on those rare occasions, she must dip beneath the surface, she needs to hold her own breath. Weightlessness and its native freedom, it scares her. No, Annie does not want to understand these depths, let alone offer them her surrender, and Tom will never again push her past those limits. She needs to be where things make sense, where she can keep control, where she can stand, breathe, float.

Of course, because Annie's floating has such an effortless appearance, this is a truth Tom sometimes forgets. When he is reminded, when here, beside the fire, he hears her voice and its tension, he instinctively wants to drop the subject. He also understands that such an abrupt change could blow Annie's cover. No one ever knows what frightens her. No one needs to know. Tom plays along. He seeks *her* surface. Above her weighty matters he drifts and locates that place where she does her carefree float. With perfect misdirection, he floats beside her.

"You know me." Tom chirps, "Nothing quite like being under water. The bass, the peacefulness, the idea that there's a place in the world where Pete can't put my nuts in his vice...I could stay there forever!"

"Tom?!" Annie glances toward Sophie. Sophie blushes, as though she has deciphered the secret meaning. "That's OK daddy." There is a long silence, a moment in which the parents are uncomfortable, but not Sophie. By now Sophie is elsewhere. Picturing her dad underwater makes her nervous. It always has. She thinks about it. She glances away. To Annie she looks embarrassed, but she is not. She is introspect, worried. Finally it is her innocent yet troubled voice that breaks the silence.

"But you always will, right dad?"

"Will what, sweetheart?"

"Come up. 'Ventually you have to come up, don't you?"

Tom knowingly smiles. He finds Sophie's eyes, holds them. "I always have, haven't I?"

She returns the smile and nods her head.

Sunset's surrender is now complete. The sky is clear, perfectly clear. Out of nowhere, a river of stars emerges and cuts a path so vivid that even those usually invisible lights now glow brightly. They are as embers scattered, ageless yet delicately fleeting. They are as sparks, a shower of silvery flashes raining around a god who into creation's first fire once pounded his hammer.

Beneath the glittering night five people are drawn together. Jen and her numbed hurt, Joe and his lonely faithfulness, Annie and her covered secrets, Sophie and her tender anxiety, Tom and his bank, each of them is sinking. It is as though they've hit quick sand and the more they struggle, the more they seek freedom, the deeper they sink. Yet the night unfolds and as it does it all seems so distant, as distant as this glittering, endless glory and the grace it confers.

Joe notices Sophie yawning and decides he will help her stay awake. He takes the child's hand and together they walk into the darkness where they find a spot and sit against a tree. In tones only she can hear, Joe tells Sophie about the big dipper and the way it points northward. He shows her Polaris, the star around which all others revolve. He swings his arm southward and with his index finger traces Orion and his belt.

Tom watches them and wonders. Is it the information, the attention he gives her, his invitingly soft tone? He cannot tell. All he knows is that Sophie is mesmerized. On Joe's every syllable, she hangs.

From a distance Jen listens. She knows the story he tells. Word for word, she can recite it. Still she listens. For a voice long unhearable, she listens. Then she too draws near and sits beside them. Sophie rests her head against Jen's side. Jen returns the gentleness, reaches around, strokes Sophie's thick curls, lightly presses her lips against Sophie's forehead. With no small sense of wonder, Joe studies Jen's face. That face, with its drawn narrowness, with its heartache etched lines, that face now possesses a distant yet familiar softness and reminds him of another time. To Joe, she is beautiful. As on their wedding day, she is beautiful. He catches Jen's eye, offers a small smile which she does not reject. It has been months, maybe longer, since he last saw this tenderness and knowing that these capacities still exist raises in him a quiet hopefulness, even a comfort.

Tom and Annie stand beside the fire. Silently she slips her hand into his, bare flesh against bare flesh, two hands becoming a single thing.

They look up.

They watch.

They all watch.

Sophie sees it first. Out of nothing it appears, a dim light that grows and brightens, then streaks, forming a downward arch that disappears into another, less distant nothing. A few seconds pass and another light appears, grows, brightens, streaks, disappears.

Then another,

and another,

and another...

This is the meteor shower that Brett, the channel 10 weather guy, promised. On the six o'clock news, Brett said that "these streaks begin as space rocks, if you can call them rocks. They are more like grains of sand, falling earthward, but never touching the ground."

They watch. Grains of sand, one after the next, glow, burn, fall, disappear. The streaks are bright and close, so close that as Sophie reaches out, she almost touches them. The moment freezes and casts the kind of spell that stops conversation. It stops everything. The injuries, the loneliness, the insecurities, the secrets, the fears; they are all stopped. For a moment, just for a moment, the bright and expansive night envelops everything. For a moment, just for a moment, the gaps that separate lovers close. For a moment, just for a moment, grains fall, but never touch the ground. They rain down, but never reach those who watch them.

They fall.

    One by one, they fall.

For a moment,

    just for a moment,

        every bit of sand into which these five people sink

            becomes a shower of light.

Of all the places that attract scuba divers, coral reefs are the most popular. To the untrained eye, the reef looks like a large rock formation that rises above the ocean floor. In truth, the corals that make the reef are living things. These animals, or coral polyps, are closely related to the jellyfish. They secrete a calcium cement that bonds them to other polyps and forms a hard skeletal structure. This structure, in turn, allows the polyps to share ingested nutrients and communicate with other colony members. Each new generation bonds itself to the skeletal structure of the last, forming layer upon layer that with each passing year grows larger and larger. The resulting ledges, holes, and hiding places provide a home for countless species, fish, coruscations, and the like.

Because it is a colony containing millions of tiny individuals, a coral reef is quite fragile. Don't forget that the reef you are diving has been growing for thousands of years. It takes so little to destroy its integrity. A good diver lives by the motto that "you are to take only pictures and leave only bubbles." It is tiny and delicate things that make these giant beauties what they are and gives many sea creatures a place to call home.

Open Water SCUBA Certification Manual
Compiled by DII (Dive Instructors International)
Pg. 16

Chapter 20

(A week and a half before the accident)

OF ALL THE HYDENS MARY Wilke has served, Tom is her favorite. In her 26 years, she has held five different Lakeland positions. She began as a teller, worked in accounting and payroll. For the last three years, Mary has been Tom's administrative assistant. Unlike Frank and Pete, Tom is as much a friend as he is a boss. He never misses birthdays, anniversaries, or children's graduations, and when her husband's cancer became un-treatable, Tom not only organized the employee vacation bank, he stepped up first, donating all his remaining PTO. For nearly three months, Mary stayed beside her husband and didn't lose so much as a quarter hour pay.

So it is that what's now happening hangs like a sickness upon her heart. She sees things she doesn't want to see. She hears things she doesn't want to hear, little things, by themselves nothings, one after the next that taken together add up to a giant, awful something. It brings her shivers. It creates in her stomach a terrible rolling that she cannot stop.

The little things: Mary has noticed lately that Tom seems preoccupied, distracted, even irritable. He arrives early, enters his office and closes the door. It is such a small thing, a nothing, but so completely out of character. Mary has asked Tom about this. She has wondered if maybe there's "trouble at home." His smile broadens. His easy way returns. He assures her that "everything at home is fine and what she sees is the product of an increased work load." He returns to his office, closes the door. Mary considers the explanation. While it is true, Tom's work load has increased, it is an unnecessary increase. He's become a micro manager, shouldering tasks that could and really should be delegated. This by itself is nothing, but given everything else…

The little things: Mary has noticed that some bank expenses have dramatically increased. She checks the ledgers. Office supplies, equipment expenditures, legal and abstracting services have all increased. He opens his door and hands her stacks of paper work. She looks through it, files it. Everything is in order. She knows that the bank is doing well, but…

The little things: Then there was the conversation. It occurred in the grocery store when Jolene, Jensen builder's bookkeeper, caught Mary's eye. It was completely innocent, the kind of familiar small talk that the meat counter so often fosters; the kids, the cold front, and their common connection, the bank.

"You know you have one dedicated boss." Jolene says.

"He's been really good to me."

"Oh, I know," Jolene replies, "but it doesn't stop there. Friday night Andy and I were on our way home from the late show and drove by the bank. Tom's car was still in the parking lot. Tom's office light was still on. 11:00 on a Friday night! Can you imagine?...Of course you can. You work with him."

Mary's heart sinks and not because Tom is working late. It sinks because in the last two weeks, this is the third time that she's heard this comment. Mary smiles, "Yes, he's really something. Thanks Jolene, I'll pass along the compliment."

Jolene walks away. Mary's smile fades. She puts it all together and wonders, "Are these random coincidences? Are they puzzle pieces?" She doesn't know.

Somewhere deep within her questions bubble, rise, surface. They are insistent questions that demand a hearing. It's heavy, sobering. She sees things she doesn't want to see. She hears things she doesn't want to hear. She wishes this would go away. Bit by bit the nothings surface and bring her to a conclusion that is both impossible and inevitable.

Something is happening. Mary can't quite say what. The something is not at all obvious, but looms like a hulking, formless giant. She sees only hints, only things that might be. Could this be just a few unrelated events, random coincidences? She hopes that it is this and not puzzle pieces. The fear that these possibilities raise create within her a black conflict. The loyalty he's so generously tendered, his deep interest in her wellbeing makes her stomach roll. Mary never would have guessed that she would question Tom's honesty, Tom's integrity. Yet this is where she finds herself, and after all Tom Hyden has done for her, these suspicions feel like a kind of betrayal, like she is stabbing a good friend. Still, something is happening.

She picks up the phone. She calls a trustee.

Chapter 21

THE ROOM'S SPARSE LIGHTING CREATES a subtle yet inviting mood. Into a nearly unseen floor, pale yellow walls disappear. Above the dozen or so raised tables, swag lamps spread gentle light. Their blue and red shades glow, painting dull splashes upon the ceiling. It is a soft ambiance that makes the room seem even smaller than it really is.

Years ago, this was a barber shop. On the walls, Sparky Erickson's original equipment is still displayed, his straight edged razors, leather straps, scissors, brushes, and hand clippers. Beside the crescent shaped bar, an old barber pole turns; the red and white helices redolent of a time when barbers were also surgeons who performed a service called bloodletting.

Although it has been centuries since barbers did surgery, the pole is apropos. Bloodletting is still practiced here. At Sparky's, Lake Pulaski long timers gather, the beer flows, and civility's proper filters disappear. Who is prospering, who is struggling, who has created their own troubles, these are all discussion topics. To be fair, there is little about these conversations that *sound* malicious. In a place like Lake Pulaski, even the whispering sports are couched in a language called *genuine concern*.

While Tom and Annie usually avoid the talk, they do enjoy the crowd and the camaraderie it provides. In this room, everyone knows everyone else. That familiarity gives one a sense of place and with it a belonging that is both blessing and bane. On one hand, people know you and care about you. On the other hand, that knowing becomes a kind of license by which those same people make your business theirs. So the regulars gather. Sparky's is buzzing. The laughter is loud and the spirit bright.

For the third time in as many weeks, Joe and Jen have begged off, an absence that, around the bar, does not go unnoticed. Tom and Annie find their usual spot and for a while sit by themselves. Soon Jeff and Meg Kingly, neighbors three doors down fill the obvious void.

"Hey Hyden, mind if we join you?" Jeff, sounds upbeat.

Tom smiles, gets up, and extends a hand, "Sure. Have a seat."

Jeff and Meg slide into the booth. Meg quietly smiles and tucks herself beneath Jeff's arm. The two of them look so happy. They always do...

"Where are the Johnsons?" Jeff continues.

"Don't know for sure," Tom replies. "Puck said something about a previous commitment."

"They're such fixtures around here. Hope everything's OK," Jeff pauses. "By the way, haven't seen much of you lately. Where have you been hiding?"

Before Tom can respond, Annie offers her own answer. "Oh, he's been a slave in brother Pete's dungeon. Some new accounting system."

"Actually, the new system is my baby." Tom adds, "Just trying to bring Lakeland into the 21st century."

"Work, work, work." Annie smiles, "Some nights I want to send a posse out after him..."

Everyone laughs, but the conversation makes Tom nervous. In truth, the new accounting system has nothing to do with Tom's long hours. He's tending the other bank, moving concealed money, generating the counterfeit paperwork that covers his tracks. When this is finished, he tinkers with procedures, double and triple checks his work, finds and corrects mistakes. Of course no one, Annie included, knows what he is really doing. So Jeff's question, Annie's little dig, it shouldn't bother him. It is just a Saturday night social and the accompanying light hearted banter,

but in it Tom hears challenge.

Tom hears accusation.

Tom hears suspicion...

He can't quite put his finger on it, but something is happening. It is not a tangible something and not something objectively identifiable. It's more like a sensation, like the world is slightly off kilter. It's subtle and it's nearly imperceptible, but something *is* happening.

The sensation reminds Tom of the Tipsy House, part of an old Iowa amusement park. As the name implies, the house is built 30 degrees from level. On the outside, the thing looks as if it could slide right off its foundation. Inside, however, where the only reference points are the perfectly squared walls, ceiling, and floors, everything looks right. Tom remembers the first time he entered the Tipsy House and the competing sensations he experienced. He remembers his eyes telling him one story, his inner ear another. He remembers walking a straight line and nearly falling over. He remembers fighting for balance, grabbing a handrail, leaning against a wall, looking through a peephole and thinking how cock-eyed the outside world appeared.

The Tipsy House was built sometime in the 20s, and is still there. Called an "illusion attraction", it is not a ride. There are no cars, no rails, no moving parts. It looks so benign, so ridiculously simple, just a place where level is not level. Yet in droves, people still come, still stagger through its perfectly squared floor plan, still laugh at the way it messes with their heads.

Tipsy, off kilter, as Tom hears Jeff and Annie, it occurs to him that this is precisely the sensation. It is, of course, not the first or only time a conversation has turned things sideways. Nearly every corner of his world has been affected. He greets customers. He goes to one of Sophie's programs and chats with other parents. He sits at Sparky's and with friends drinks his beer. Outwardly, nothing has changed. These encounters are still perfectly squared, same topics, same people, same everything. Yet lately everything seems wrong. At work, he watches other employees watch him. He wonders, "Have they always watched me like this?" He doesn't know. He talks with old friends and longtime acquaintants, but everything they say makes him suspicious. He wonders if their words carry double meanings, if they're mining for information, if they suspect that something's up. Then there's Annie. He's short with Annie! She says the same things she has always said, carries herself the same way she has always carried herself. It's nothing new. In fact, these are the very things about her that he used to find endearing, but now they sound transparently breezy and it bugs the hell out of him.

He looks people in the eye, but finds he can't. He tries to be what he has always been, but it doesn't work. He pays honest compliments, extends a hand of genuine friendship, says things and means them, but the words sound cheap, insincere and he doesn't know why. Maybe it's just him and the way his secrets keep him edgy. Maybe it's just a case of irrational over sensitivity, or maybe it's because Tom's base honesty, being who he appears to be, is no longer possible and it taints even a simple "good morning". When this happens, when people think you are one thing, but you've become something else, everything they say smacks of accusation and nothing you say sounds real.

This is what Tom is now experiencing. Even when the situation has nothing to do with the bank or the flipping of numbers, Tom hears himself and his words sound contrived. He finds that the truth, even when it *is* the truth, sounds like lies, and lies sound like the truth.

This is what's so odd. Everything is wrong, but by all appearances things have never looked this right. Money has never been this right. The pressures, bill paying, reshuffling his envelope piles, leaving the *unknown number* phone calls unanswered are all gone. Tom no longer watches helplessly as Annie makes another Des Moines run. He no longer lays awake and listens as the envelopes sound their grim litany, as they voice their accusations. This is all gone, completely gone.

Yes, everything is wrong.

No, things have never looked this right.

Something *is* happening. Gravity is exerting unexpected forces. Everything his eyes confirm as truth tips. He stands, but cannot keep upright. The walls, floor, and ceiling are square, but not level and he looks around to find something, anything that will give him a sense of up or down, right or wrong, but reality is tipsy. Living with the constant suspicion, his devalued small talk, Tom becoming what he has always abhorred, maybe this is the real cost of doing business.

So, Tom goes to work. He arrives early. He stays late. He's tired. He's irritable. He sounds phony. He staggers around every room he enters and hopes he's the only one who notices. He peers through peepholes and wonders how the outside world could be so slanted. He wishes he could tell Annie, explain this sacrifice, show her the real Thomas Hyden, but of course he can't. After all, there is no more Thomas Hyden. That man is gone.

Chapter 22

...Jeff and Meg slide into the booth. Meg quietly smiles and tucks herself beneath Jeff's arm. The two of them look so happy. They always do...

IT LOOKS AS IF THINGS are again settled, as if the two of them have completely recovered and their little setback is now just a distant memory.

It was three maybe four years ago. Meg Kingly wandered. No one knows precisely what happened, no one, not friends, not family, not Jeff, and if you were to now ask her, probably not even Meg could say for certain. After all, life for the Kinglys was so settled that leaving the way she did didn't add up. At the time, Jeff and Meg had just celebrated their eleventh anniversary. It was a stable marriage. They had a nice home and two children. Jeff was a wonderful provider and there were no apparent money troubles. By all accounts, including Meg's own, Jeff was a good husband and doting father. Meg wasn't looking, or so she claimed. She was content, or so she seemed. Everything was...*settled*. It didn't add up.

She just wandered.

His name was Doug Newman. Those who knew Doug could not say what happened, no one, not friends, not family, not Sandy, his wife. He just wandered. Meg and Doug had nothing in common except that they worked in the same office and somehow they landed in each other's arms.

When it happened, the fall was completely unstoppable. For Meg and Doug, it felt like some irresistible law of nature had exerted itself, sucking them into an inescapable vortex.

For the rest of the immediate world, it looked as if a strange madness had descended upon them both, a madness that made passion the center of their universe and rendered everything else meaningless. Into this most unlikely affair, Meg and Doug flung themselves and did so without reservation. There was not so much as a moment of uncertainty, no wondering if this was the right thing, no second guessing, and no weighing of consequences. Nothing. They each packed a suitcase, went to their respective spouses, announced their intentions, and left.

Of course, there *were* consequences the reach of which was something that Meg completely miscalculated. Oh yes, she fully expected that Jeff would have difficulty, and he did. She expected that her children might reject her, and they did. She also, however, expected that the rest of her relationships and the rest of Doug's relationships would remain essentially unchanged and when this did *not* happen, when in fact Meg and Doug became Lake Pulaski pariahs, it completely blindsided her.

They were both ostracized, but especially Meg. Everyone shunned her. Everyone. Rock solid friends would not speak to her. Her parents disowned her. Even Meg's inside circle shut her down.

To Meg, this rejection and the ensuing abandonment was completely befuddling. It made no sense. Distant acquaintances saw her at the grocery store or in the coffee shop and walked the other way. Phone calls were left unreturned. Party invitations, shopping trips, impromptu wine gatherings all dried up. For many of those who spurned her, their only connection to Jeff was through Meg. These were *her* friends and she thought she could count on their understanding, their support, even their compassion. She was wrong. Not only were such sympathies totally absent, but the treatment she received became almost scornful.

Truth be known, Meg was not cavalier as much as she was naive.

Naiveté. Meg *really* believed that friendship would and should trump everything else, including this indiscretion. It never occurred to her that even the most casual of friendships are always predicated upon an assumed, nearly invisible, honesty. Thus when Meg left Jeff, when the honesty was discarded and it became clear that Meg was not the wife, the mother, the person she pretended to be, that nearly invisible foundation began crumbling.

Naiveté. Meg *really* believed that her affair was a private matter and that other than Jeff and her girls no one else could or should claim a stake. It never occurred to her that when nearly invisible foundations start crumbling, even the most casual of friendships have a way of becoming casualties. For eleven years Meg said she was Jeff's wife. For eight of those years she said she was Molly and Maci's devoted mom. What she didn't understand is that when it comes to everything else and everyone else, being who you say you are matters. Even if it is just the grade school ride pool, in which Meg takes her turn moving kids, or the book club, or the coffee moms, or her golf league, or the weekend couples gatherings, people extend friendship based on who you say you are.

People make themselves vulnerable based on who you say you are. People even choose exercise buddies or meet for a beer based on who you say you are. Who you say you are matters, and when suddenly it is discovered that the trust this webbing promises is ill founded, is made of brittle, easily breakable synthetics, everyone who has cradled even a small portion of their life there feels betrayed.

Naiveté. Meg *really* believed that her friends had become "sanctimonious", "holier than thou". While of course there *was* plenty of venomous condescension, much of what Meg read to be judgmental was, in fact, something very different. Her friends felt betrayed and Meg's actions damaged them. What she thought she heard to be sanctimony was in fact anger-covered hurt and while those sentiments carry with them a judgmental tone, while they sound spiteful, or they attack with a vengeance, such things are really nothing more than expressions of that hurt.

The affair, which lasted less than a year, ended as abruptly and unceremoniously as it began. One day Meg packed her suitcase, went to Doug, announced her intentions, and returned home. Friends told Jeff that he should not take her back. They warned him that since she had shown her true colors, she should never again be trusted. Jeff, on the other hand, had children to raise and the mother those children so needed was standing at his doorstep. He also claimed that he still loved her, which was absolutely true. He took her back. They met with their pastor who sent them to a family therapist. They worked things out. Time passed. Friends and family watched. The signs were all good. It looked as though between them a fire had rekindled. People saw them walking hand in hand through the mall, frequenting Sparky's, catching a movie, out for dinner. People saw them finding a corner table, smiling, whispering, sharing a quiet meal. People saw them reconnecting and as they watched this, one by one the strands of brittle synthetics were replaced with more trusting fibers. Over time, Meg's other relationships renewed themselves, began to stabilize. Jeff trusted her. Her friends did the same. Meg was again what she said she was. Everything was back to normal.

...Jeff and Meg slide into the booth. Meg quietly smiles and tucks herself beneath Jeff's arm. The two of them look so happy. They always do...

Or so it seems...

To this day, Jeff cannot forget what has happened. Oh he has tried, but he cannot. Between the two of them there has developed a bitter resentment, a barrier that no one else sees. When they are alone, they do not speak. There is no sharing, no intimacy. It has become a loveless marriage. For his part, Jeff would do anything to forget. Anything. The years pass until finally he has resigned himself to the fact that as long as he is with Meg, the betrayal will never go away. So he tells himself that he stays for the children, but that is not the whole of it. There is another reason he stays. Jeff has become comfortable with bitterness. Like an old shirt, the hurt and its sourness forms itself around him. Without it, Jeff feels naked, incomplete, even defenseless. He blames Meg. He hates himself. He wants to rise above it. Again he tries, but does not know how. In public all is well.

In private things are icy,
    so icy,
        so hurt-filled.

Chapter 23

THREE AND A HALF WEEKS and not a dozen words have passed between them. Jen has been avoiding Joe. They are not eating together. They share the bed, but do not touch, thus creating a wide, deep canyon-like impasse. After a day of work, Joe comes home and cannot find Jen. She's downstairs folding laundry. She's weeding the garden. She's grocery shopping, errand running. She is just missing. Joe wants a conversation. He wants to know what's wrong, but Jen smothers every opportunity. She gets up early. She goes to bed late. She's gone.

Tonight is different. At the kitchen table Jen sits, waits. She is nervous, but has not been drinking. For this conversation, she needs a clear head.

Until recently, things had been better. Until recently, Joe noticed that her whiskey breath had all, but disappeared. They had resumed many of the activities that once marked a normal life, dinner with friends, movie dates, bonfires, Saturday nights at Sparky's. They'd even made love a few times. While clearly Jen was still guarded, still distant, their relationship had found a small piece of level ground.

Then something happened. Joe was taking his morning shower and his phone buzzed. "Ribbet, ribbet." Joe had mentioned that he was waiting for a call, but when she picked up his phone, she saw that it wasn't a call, but a text. Someone named Kelly had written two simple words.

"Coffee's on…"

This was not "Kelly's" only message. How many were there? 60? 100? More? She couldn't tell. She scrolled back. Some were running conversations, others a single communication.

"He's being a pain in the, butt."

"I'm tired of living this way."

"Taking the boys to school. Meet U in 15."

"Everyone's so stinking phony."

"TnkU."

"You're the only friend I have."

It hits Jen. This Kelly has her own ring tone!

She thinks back. Over the last few months how many times has she heard the frog's call? How many times has Joe checked his phone, pushed a button, slid it into his pocket? She can't remember.

The phone buzzed. Right in her hand it buzzed! It startled Jen! "Ribbit, ribbit." "Kelly", whoever the hell Kelly is, was this close…

Jen checks the message.

"?"

She hears Joe turn off the shower. Quickly Jen put the phone back where she found it…and said nothing.

That was three and a half weeks ago. Ever since she has watched him, noticed his habits, listened for the signal. The frog would croak. He'd check other messages, but never the frog, at least never in Jen's presence.

"Someone need you?"

"Just a customer."

He'd wait. He'd leave the room. He'd run an errand. Through the blinds she'd watch him as he'd dig in his pocket, scroll through his messages, find "Kelly's" little nothings.

At the kitchen table Jen sits, waits. Joe walks through the door. He holds a stack of envelopes, today's mail. Her presence surprises him, but he does not show it. At first nothing is said, no greetings, no acknowledgments, no eye contact. There is just a tense silence, which Jen finally breaks.

"So where have you been?"

"Des Moines."

She gets up, goes to the cupboard. Glass.

    Cupboard to the fridge. Ice.

        Fridge to the cabinet. Coke. Jack. More Jack than Coke.

"Want one?" Joe says nothing, nods. She repeats the process and sets his glass on the table. There is no hiding Jack. Directly between them he sits.

"I know about you, about the two of you."

Joe looks puzzled. Jen drops a hint. "Coffee's on?"

"Kelly?"

Jen nods her head and repeats his answer. "Kelly."

"What in the world do you think you know?" Joe asked.

"Oh nothing, just a little coffee and whatever else comes with it."

"Now wait, Jen. I have nothing to hide." Joe is passionately matter of fact, "This is not what you think. We started having coffee a few months ago, back when you and I were having a rough time.

I swear to you, it is a friendship, nothing more. Jen, don't you know that you are my only interest? I love you and everything I do is for you, *only* for you. Even coffee with Kelly keeps me focused on you. I wouldn't touch anyone else. I wouldn't. I cou..." Joe pauses, looks into the table. "It's just that...you know, you've stuffed yourself in that bottle for so damned long that I finally...I had to talk about this with someone. I had to get my head straight and Kelly helped me. She was a safe place to process things."

"What do you mean, safe?"

"Just what I said. Safe. This is also why I can tell you that I have nothing to hide."

Jen rests the glass against her mouth and tips her head back. The ice rattles then slides, touching her upper lip. She says nothing.

"So here we are again. Why don't you get yourself out of that stinking bottle." Joe's voice projects an uncharacteristic emotion, a mix of frustration and desperation. "It's killing us, Jen. We won't last long this way."

Jen wraps her fingers around Jack's neck and pours another. She tips the bottle toward Joe, as if to ask, "Want one?" Joe ignores the gesture. "This isn't about me. This is about you and your little friend. Besides, I can quit anytime I want."

"No you can't and you know it. You drink alone. You're missing work, lots of it. You're sleeping all the time. Do you think I haven't noticed?"

Jen's response is monotone, apathetic. "You're not my mother."

"Call me what you want. You need help and most of all you need me."

"You're wrong, mom. I don't need you and I don't care. I don't care what you do. I don't care who you see. I don't care about any of it."

"If you don't care, then why bring it up?"

The observation sets Jen back. She looks into her glass, recalculates. "That's a good question. Why don't you just leave? It's time for you to go. Just...go."

"No," His voice becomes firm, defiant. "I'm not going anyplace." The tone and its accompanying resolve surprises him. From deep within him a familiar posture raises and brings a hopefulness. He hopes his resistance will piss her off. He hopes she'll flash a long repressed anger, tell him to "get the hell out", grab his arm and pull him to the door. He hopes his provocation will bring the storm he knows she's hiding, that her rage will violently blow, and her hurt will thunder, and finally, *finally* all of that which, for the last few years, has tormented her will come spilling out.

"Hell no," Defiance becomes emphatic. Joe stakes his ground.

Jen shows only bland indifference. She reaches for Jack. On top of the second she pours a third. "Suit yourself." She grabs the remote, flips on the television, looks away.

A couple of years ago, Joe would have seen this for what it is, Jen's final protest, a prelude to surrender. A couple of years ago, he would have taken the bottle and poured the whiskey down the toilet. He would have stood between Jen and the television, blocked her view. He would have goaded her until she could hide no longer, but he doesn't do any of this. Her voice carries no anger and her eyes no passion. The fires which once drove her seem completely extinguished. She says she does not care and by every outward measure, Jen speaks the truth.

So Joe is left standing there. It pains him. It hurts like hell, but he is at a complete loss. He doesn't want to leave. He wants to stay and fight. He squares up, ready to deliver another salvo, but finds that he doesn't know how. Through it all, Jen has become completely impervious. Engaging her is like hitting tennis balls against a mattress. With no other options, Joe gets up, walks toward the door.

Out of the corner of her eye, Jen sees him leave. She doesn't want him to go, she wants him to stay. In fact, she wants to kick his ass. Like a boiling pot, her rage is rising, bubbling to the surface, surging. With all her strength, she holds it back. She hears the door close. She takes a long gulp, turns back to the television. What's on the tube? She doesn't know and doesn't care. All she can say is that she wishes he would stay. She wants to chase him down, but knows she can't.

Her life, she has decided, is like drifted snow packed against a mountain slope. Precariously it hangs above her, and she knows that once she starts poking around, loosening that hardened drift even a little bit, the ensuing avalanche will bury her. No, she doesn't want him to go. She wants to fight with him. She wants to fight *for* him. She wants to again have him as her own, but she can't, she just can't. So, she watches him walk and as she does, Jen feels an ache that not even Jack can dull.

Joe gets in his pickup. He holds the key, but cannot find the ignition. He glances around the steering wheel, but cannot see. Moisture fills his eyelids, spills over the rim, and then cascades around his cheeks and down his neck. The tears cool him, producing a shiver. The shiver, in turn, becomes a shaking, violent and not controllable. He doesn't know what to do with himself. He doesn't know where to turn. Everything is a blur. He thinks about his parents, his child. He feels that all the things in his world that meant something are now gone. He wants to go someplace, but there is nowhere to go. Nowhere. The night and its blackness penetrate him. It is all so very black.

    He sits in his truck.

        He holds the key.

           He can't see.

Chapter 24

Jen,

I woke up this morning and had a premonition that something terrible was going to happen, and that maybe by the end of the day I wouldn't be here anymore. I've never had that feeling before, certainly nothing that intense...scared the crap out of me.

It used to be that you'd wrap yourself around me and this kind of stuff would disappear. We used to lie together and in those moments everything seemed so right. You probably don't know this, but you had a way of lifting me, and it was a lifting that reached to the deepest places of my heart. I don't know why I never tell you this stuff. I don't know why I sometimes act like such a jerk. I don't know anything anymore except that all we seem capable of doing is ignoring each other. It used to be that you'd fix me and then the other shoe would drop. It used to be that I'd make you feel good only to later screw things up and you'd get hurt worse than before. That's how it worked for us. Fix and hurt. Hurt and fix. It wasn't perfect, but it was good, really good. Now? I don't know what's happened. We try to connect and can't. We try some more and can't. It's like a dull, heartless movie that keeps replaying itself and maybe it's time to end the trying. I wish I had the answers. I don't.

I stopped by the house this morning and collected a few things. I don't know where I'll go. It doesn't really matter. I'll see to it that nothing will change for you, at least not in where you'll live. How you live, who you live with is another matter.

Maybe this is the terrible thing of my premonition. I don't know.

Joe

Chapter 25

TOM HANGS HIS COAT, OPENS the shades, starts his computer listens to his voicemail. The third message stops him. "Mr. Hyden, this is Dennis Fisher from Criminal Investigation, State of Iowa. Would you please give me a call? 515-331-3416."

Tom leans back, runs a hand over his pant pocket, feels the jump drive. He thinks, "Maybe this is nothing." He knows better. The computer screen looks unfocused. He begins reading yesterday's summary, but the font has become small and he can no longer see the numbers.

The phone sits on his desk and looks as if it is waiting. Tom wonders what this Fisher guy knows, and decides that there is only one way to find out.

"Mr. Fisher. This is Tom Hyden returning your call." His tone is upbeat, almost Annie-like.

"Mr. Hyden. Thank you for calling. I was wondering if I could have a few minutes of your time."

"Of course. My morning is wide open."

"Great. I'm finishing up a few things here. 10 o'clock?"

"10 o'clock." Tom repeats the time, hangs up.

It is a long hour and a half, very long. Although he's never met the man, the name Dennis Fisher is familiar. Tom has heard it countless times, most recently in connection with an arson investigation. Just a few weeks ago Fisher had proven that a Cedar Rapids couple intentionally set their failing restaurant afire and then collected an insurance settlement. When that story broke, Tom didn't give it much thought. Now it seems invasive, almost personal. Now this same Fisher is calling him? This is not some local cop who wants an auto loan quote. No, this is different and Tom finds that he cannot think. He closes his eyes and re-maps the entire operation, the Bank of Tom business loans, the ledgers on which those loans are tracked, the dummy vendor accounts, the fictitious paper trails. Until this moment, he regarded his work as a massive accomplishment and it gave him an odd sense of pride. The deception was, in fact, so beautifully crafted that he'd even dared to believe that he could manage it forever, and even though he wondered about others and what they might know, he could explain his *Tipsy House* suspicions as healthy paranoia. This, however, is different. Fisher's call makes him feel naked and he wonders how soon before the entire world sees the lump in his pocket and its awful secrets. He imagines the meeting that will soon take place. He imagines how quickly and easily this meeting could disturb all the silt that has for so long rested beneath his dark yet perfect clarity. One thing is certain, Tom needs to see what Fisher sees. A plan emerges. He will watch Fisher. He will listen, but not speak. He will keep his cool, appear cooperative.

The entire bank tilts, more than usual. Mary looks tightly wound. The normal office chatter seems muted. Tom wonders,

"Is everyone looking at him, peeking around their computer monitors, stealing a glance? Do they know something he doesn't?" He can't say.

    8:47.

        9:12.

            9:36.

He counts the minutes. He wants this behind him.

    9:54.

Even though Tom has never seen Dennis Fisher he immediately spots him. Fisher is tall, athletic, wearing khakis and a blue polo. His first stop is the front desk. The receptionist smiles, her lips move, but there is no sound. She points, gives directions. Fisher returns her smile, nods.

"Mr. Fisher? Thomas Hyden. Nice to meet you." The two men shake hands. Tom motions to a chair and sits behind his desk. "So. What brings you to our bank? Setting up an account? Maybe a mortgage?"

"No, I wish I could say I was." Fisher gets right to the point. "Unfortunately I'm here on official business. It has come to my attention that Lakeland's books contain some irregularities and I've been asked to conduct an investigation."

The office suddenly goes dark and all clarity vanishes. Panic rises. Tom instinctively slows his breathing, considers his options. Since he needs to see what Fisher sees, there is no other choice, he plays along, the conversation follows its own course.

"Irregularities?" Tom sounds surprised.

"Yes," Fisher continues, "I really don't know too much yet. In fact, I may find that there's nothing wrong. That's why I've been called in and, of course, I'm only beginning. There's a long way to go here. Over the next few weeks, I'll be in and out of the bank, collecting information and interviewing several key employees. I'm hoping to start with you. So Mr. Hyden, may I call you Tom?" Tom nods. "If you're willing, I'd like to ask a few questions, but before I start, I want you to know that you don't have to talk to me." Again Tom nods. "And if it's ok, I'd like to record our conversation."

Fisher's comment, "...*you don't have to talk to me...*", raises a vague anxiety. Tom wonders, "Is this the kind of thing Fisher would say only to those who will soon be accused, or is this how he begins every interview?" Tom leans back, further slows his breathing, relaxes his body.

"Of course. And I want you to know that I will help however I can."

"Great." Fisher smiles, sets his recorder on the desk. "First tell me a bit about yourself." He motions to the pictures on the desk. "You must have a family."

Tom gives the recorder a glance, looks away. He opens his mouth and is surprised at how normal he sounds. This settles him, centers him. "Yes, that's Annie, my wife. We've been married for thirteen years...and then there's Sophie. She's almost nine."

"What a good looking family. You must be very proud of them."

"Yes, I am. I love my family. They are my reason. Everything I do is for Annie and Sophie."

"Got a family myself," Fisher smiles, "I know what you mean. It's like the sun rises and sets on them." Tom nods in agreement. "So where do you live?"

"314 St. Andrews Drive."

"Oh...Nice. You must golf."

"No, I'm not much of a golfer...do it only when I have to. Annie wanted to live on the course, kind of a status thing, you know. She has a bunch of friends out there, and she loves the view out the back window. I have to say that it's grown on me too."

"That's wonderful. You've got a job that allows you to provide for her like this." Fisher pauses, jots a couple of notes. "So Mr. Hyden...Tom. As I'd mentioned earlier, the books here contain some irregularities."

"What do you mean by irregularities, what are you seeing?"

"Well, I'm no expert so I really can't say for sure. In the next few weeks, I hope to be learning more. In fact, I'll be counting on people like you. With your business background, I'm hoping you can help me understand how the bank keeps its records. In that regard, it looks like loan accounts are being shorted and the money just disappears. I was hoping maybe you could tell me a bit about Lakeland's bookkeeping. Have you ever noticed anything that might look questionable or maybe bookkeeping problems that could easily be missed or hidden? And if you do, how are such short falls discovered? I'm assuming you have some kind of check and balance system, right?"

"There is, but I'm not sure I know what you're talking about. I think we've got some pretty clean accounting practices here. About the only thing I ever see are occasional input errors."

"Tell me about this, Mr. Hyden. How are mistakes made? How are they discovered and corrected?"

"It's pretty simple," Tom is now completely at ease. He has practiced this speech a thousand times. "Say for instance, a customer makes a payment of $950, but payment is entered as $590. This is called a numbers transposition and it's more common than you might think. In fact, when the books don't balance this is one of the first places we look."

"I see. Who inputs these payments?"

"Oh, tellers, loan officers, their assistants, nearly everyone who works here."

"And when you find these mistakes, what happens and when does it happen?"

"To my knowledge, mistakes are almost always caught. Sometimes it takes a few days, but we find the error...by we, I mean our accounting department. As soon as the error is discovered, the appropriate credit is then issued and the customer's account is corrected."

"And you're in charge of that department, right?"

"Yes. Of course." Tom pauses. "You don't think one of my people is stealing from the bank, do you?"

"It appears that way, but I don't know?" Fisher replies. "As I said earlier, this is the beginning of a long investigation and, in the end, I may find that the books are clean and everything is just fine. It's hard to say. Along the way, I'll be talking with a number of people. While we're on the subject, is it ok to talk with your wife?"

"Annie? Why would you want to talk with her?..." Tom doesn't wait for an answer. "No...no she's a bit of a worrier and knows absolutely nothing about the bank. If there's some problem, I'd prefer to handle her myself."

"Sure Mr. Hyden. I understand. After all, it is your family's business. What is this, the third generation of Hydens running the bank?" Tom smiles, holds up four fingers. "Oh." Fisher corrects himself, "Four. I'm sure that image...the integrity of your family name is very important."

Tom nods his agreement, pauses, asks, "So if you find that someone is taking money, what will you do to...I mean what will happen with that person?" Tom has not practiced this question, but it is the only thing on his mind. He listens to himself ask and the question sounds wrong. He feels like he's just exposed himself, but the words are already released.

If Tom has telegraphed his discomfort, Fisher doesn't seem to notice. "Should the investigation uncover wrong doing, I'll have to move pretty quickly. There will be a warrant issued. As soon as this happens, we will find the accused and arrest him or her. Then the matter goes to the district attorney and everyone prepares for a trial."

"I see," Tom slows, checks his gauges, sees the situation, returns to his script. "This is just so hard to believe. We're all like family here. One of them stealing. I just...just can't imagine it."

"Well, I hope you're right. It's always a sad thing." Fisher pauses, checks his notes, "Unless you have something to add, I think this covers things for now."

Tom makes a gesture, as if to say, "I've nothing else," and stands up. Fisher closes his notebook, pockets his recorder, and shakes Tom's hand.

Dennis Fisher is gone. The dark clarity returns and Tom relaxes. He knows this shouldn't be happening, but his confidence rises and swells. The meeting with Fisher went better than he expected. Still he is wary. Over the next several nights, sleep comes in small increments. He goes to work and does nothing. He is and is not with Annie. Only the Bank of Tom receives his full attention. He checks his procedures. He reviews the deception and everything about it that by nature remains visible. There is a scrutiny he hopes he won't face, but knows he will. He prepares for it.

Chapter 26

THE HYDENS WALK PAST THEIR usual spot and sit more toward the front. On a normal Sunday, the first several pews are empty, but today is Bible Presentation and the church is packed. Fourth graders and their parents have come early, secured choice seating. A few families, like the Hydens, are regular attenders. Most, however, come only on high holidays or occasions such as this. The children are noisy and well dressed. Parents are smiling, expressionless, proud, bored, happy, wishing they were somewhere else. A few have brought their video equipment. After the first hymn, Pastor Cathy will read the names and as she does, the fourth graders will come forward. She will give a short talk, then one by one the students will receive their first Bibles.

Joe and Jen are not far behind and take the spots Annie saved for them. It has been months since either have worshiped. With all the recent troubles, church feels uncomfortable and the events of the past week have reinforced this undiscussed decision. The night Jen asked him to leave, Joe moved into the Hyden's basement. This was not his intention. He came by, just needing an ear, and Tom insisted that he stay. For Annie this has been a hardship. Not that Joe is a bother. In fact, having him around is easy. No, Annie is simply worried. Lately, Jen has been invisible and Joe's nightly presence not only makes that invisibility unavoidable, but puts Annie in an awkward position. Twice this week she has stopped by the Johnson house, rang the doorbell, but never made a connection. She doesn't know if Jen is not home or if Jen is not answering.

Today there is only one reason that the two of them are together. For Sophie, they will set their problems aside. They need to see their goddaughter receive her Bible. They meet outside, walk in together. Jen is happy to see Joe. Joe is happy to see Jen. Neither admits it. Neither lets it show. The moment is both good and awkward. They sit. Sophie clutches her Bible. They smile and listen to the preacher.

Pastor Cathy tells about Sammy, her two year old Brittany. "One day last spring ol' Sammy ran off. He was just gone. We looked everywhere, but Sammy could not be found. We walked the neighborhood. We drove around. It took hours, but finally we spotted him. Sammy had wandered over a mile away, clear out on the edge of town. He was wet, hungry, and oh so frightened, and when finally I saw him and how scared he was I knew what had happened. He didn't run away. He was just doing what came naturally, he followed his nose. One scent led to another, to another, to another until he couldn't find his way home. In fact, I'm sure that, for the longest time, he didn't even know he was lost. He was just doing what Brittanys do. He was just following his nose."

"Isn't that how it is with us?" Cathy continues, "We get lost... and it's not that we're doing anything particularly wrong or bad.

We just do what comes naturally and, in the process, get ourselves all turned around. We get buried in our busy lives, make our great plans and pursue our big ambitions. We collect our riches and build our image meanwhile our families become strangers. We get lost. We get lost in our hurts, finding that sometimes the pain is so great that we can't see anything else. We get lost when someone does us wrong and we can't let it go. We get lost..."

"And like I said, it's not that we're doing anything wrong. No, we're just following our nose, just doing what everyone expects of us, but the end result is that we get so far in the weeds that we lose our way...

"So..." Pastor Cathy pauses, "Isn't it time to come home? Isn't it time to find your way back, find where you've come from, and the people you love, and the things in life that are true. Isn't it time? Come home." She says. "Come home."

Pastor Cathy has everyone stand. The organist plays the prelude. The hymn sing begins. This is Sophie's favorite part of the week. She's almost nine years old and still she stands on the pew, leans against her mom, listens. In her college choir, Annie was the soprano section leader, a gift that over the years has not diminished. Her voice soars high above all others. She sings improvised descants and Sophie thinks that this must be how the angels sound. Sophie listens. She presses herself closer, wraps her arm around Annie's waist, holds her tightly, covers her other ear so that all she can hear is her mother's voice and all its unearthly beauty. The two of them are close, so close that Sophie can feel Annie's chest resonating against her own. It is as if the two of them are one and Sophie imagines that if she could just get a little closer that she could understand, maybe even become that perfectly beautiful thing.

Come home, come home. Come ho-o-ome. Ye who are weary come ho-o-ome.

Softly and tenderly Jesus is calling, calling us sinners come home.

Of course no one knows why Sophie does this. For Tom, seeing Annie accepting Sophie always pleases him. Annie, on the other hand has, for some time been uncomfortable with it. When Sophie was five, six, even seven it was cute and Annie would gladly return the kindness, wrap her arm over Sophie's shoulder and lean into her so that one supported the other, but not today. Annie has decided that Sophie needs to grow up and Bible Sunday provides the perfect occasion. Today Annie gently slides an arm between them, prying Sophie away from her. She opens a hymn book and puts it into Sophie's hands. She extends an index finger and helps Sophie follow the music. "You just got your first Bible," Annie whispers, "You're a big girl now."

Sophie's shoulders relax, slump. She slips off the pew and stands beside her mother. Although she snuggles in as closely as she can, it is not the same. The voice, that heavenly voice is still there, still soaring, but now the distance between Sophie and that beautiful thing is greater than ever. Sophie is afraid that she will never again feel Annie's song resonate against her body, that she will never penetrate its mysteries or divine its lovely secrets.

Tom tenses, looks straight ahead.

The drive home is uncomfortably quiet. Annie starts a conversation, but Tom offers no replies. Finally they get home, Sophie goes off to play and the two of them are alone. Tom confronts Annie. His voice is quiet, but so intense that the anger it suppresses is not containable. "Why did you do that, push her away like that?"

"Well it's time for her to be a big girl. She needs to follow the service. She needs to open..."

Tom doesn't let her finish. "Don't do that. Don't ever do that. She needs you. Don't you get it? She looks up to you. She thinks she's never good enough and you're the only one who can fix that! What happens if I'm not here to protect her from this crap? You're it!..." Tom stops, tries to continue, but can't. "You're it!!!"

Annie doesn't know what to say. She has never seen him this way. Oh yes, from time to time he gets testy, but nothing like this. It is a visceral anger and it so shocks Annie that she doesn't know what to say. She says nothing. She retreats, waits all afternoon for an apology she knows will come.

It never does.

Annie has noticed that lately Tom has been preoccupied, distant. After a day at work, he comes home, but it is like he is someplace else. She asks him about work. She knows that Pete drives him crazy. He used to share his day, but not lately. "Everything's fine," he says. "Keeping my head above water." "Doing the deal..." He drops these one liners, deflects her concern, smiles and withdraws. Yes, she's known that he's under some pressure, but now this? This incident comes as a complete surprise.

Afternoon turns to evening. Tom cleans the garage, mulches leaves, fixes a gutter. For a long time, Annie watches him, waits for him to come inside. He doesn't. She fixes two glasses of lemonade, delivers them.

"Honey something's up. What's wrong? You've not been yourself."

Tom takes her hand, pulls her close, whispers, "Just treat her right, Annie. Always treat her right." Then he kisses her on the cheek and says, "You know I love you both." The anger is gone, but the intensity remains. There is an urgency to his tone and it frightens Annie.

She wants to understand.
   She wants to ask more.
      She does not.

Chapter 27

THE ROOM HAS NO WINDOWS, no pictures, and, save a small table, an office chair, and a straight back chair, no furniture. The receptionist has brought Tom here, offered him the straight back chair, and told him that "Officer Fisher will be just a moment."

The room's emptiness creeps around and through him. Earlier that morning Fisher called, told Tom that "...The investigation is progressing, but I have a few more questions..." Now Tom waits. They set an 11:00 meeting. It is 11:16. The chair in which he sits has no arms. It is hard, uncomfortable. The room's austerity, the wait, the table pushed against the wall, the door cracked open, nothing about this is right. Tom feels naked. He wants to get up, walk out the door, go someplace where he feels less exposed, but he doesn't know where that might be. So he sits. Waits.

Fisher enters. In his left hand, he holds a blue hanging folder. The folder is about an inch thick and contains a hodgepodge of loose papers, different sizes, different colors. Tom instinctively gets up, but Fisher raises his right hand, signaling Tom to remain seated. Tom sits, Fisher stands over him. His 6' 2" frame is imposing and only increases the discomfort.

"Mr. Hyden." Fisher's voice is dispassionate, matter of fact, "I appreciate your willingness to come. I won't take much of your time and like I said in our first meeting, you are free to go. The doors are open and if you don't want to stay, no one is forcing you." Fisher pauses, wiggles the file up and down, using it as a pointer. "However we have some things to talk about."

He takes the office chair and lays the file aside. Barely two feet separate the men. For Tom, this is far too close. He wants to retreat. He wants to recover lost personal space. The chair legs grip the floor. He feels trapped.

Fisher continues. "I have concluded my investigation and I believe that you are responsible."

Tom's reaction is instinctive. He leans toward Fisher, making himself as big as possible, "That's a lie and you..." Fisher turns his head away from Tom and puts up a hand. The hand is large, powerful, like that of a traffic cop. Just as a single hand stops a lane of cars, so this hand stops Tom. Without touching him, it halts Tom's attack, deflects his words, forces a retreat. Into his seat, into his chair back, that hand pushes Tom back.

Fisher holds the pose, waits. Slowly he turns his head. Slowly he lowers his hand. He looks over the hand, studies Tom's face, his arms, his feet, his posture. Tom thinks Fisher sees him break eye contact, sees his shoulders roll downward, sees his index finger tapping against his pant leg, sees the artery in his neck rapidly pulsing. Tom thinks Fisher sees everything.

"I need to talk to my lawyer..."

The hand goes back up, repels another sentence, stops another advance. When it is lowered, Fisher matter-of-factly states, "I can't give you legal advice, however we still have some things to talk about...Listen, Mr. Hyden. I've done a thorough investigation. I've worked the case hard, talked to everyone. Now I want to get the truth. I want you to tell me the truth." There is another pause that seems longer than the first. Fisher rolls his office chair toward Tom, leans forward. They are now just inches apart, their knees almost touching. Tom again tries backing away, but his chair will not slide. "The truth is sometimes hard..." Fisher's lowered voice trails off. He waits for a response, gets none.

There is another pause. His tone changes, softens. "See this pencil? Do you know why it has an eraser?... Because sometimes people make mistakes..." His voice is now almost a whisper. It carries empathy, understanding. "Tom, I know you've been living above your means. I know Annie wants nice things and you want to give them to her. Listen, you're not a hardened criminal. I know that. You're not pointing guns at people or abusing children, but you've just gotten yourself into a situation here. I understand. It makes sense...You had to save your family. You had to make things right, pay the bills, keep the roof over their heads, give Annie the things you knew she deserved. I've got a family too. I know. I understand."

Tom looks away. Fisher reaches over, places a gentle hand on Tom's knee. The touch is not accusing, not threatening, not invasive. It is deeply human, aesculapian, like the man behind the touch is reaching out, seeking a connection. It touches him. It comes to rest not on Tom's knee, but his troubled heart. "It's over, Tom." Fisher whispers, "It's time to erase the mistake. It's time to tell me the truth."

Tom shudders. He is utterly defeated and does not know what is next. He thinks about Annie, Sophie. He thinks about his mom, his dad. He thinks about the Hyden name. He thinks about Eldo and how he is again silted in, can't see a damned thing. He needs time. More time. He remembers the dive reel, the safety line and the unseen exit to which it is attached. He had always hoped it wouldn't come to this, but now knows that if he's going to follow that line and escape this mess, he'll need to find a place where the water is clear and things make sense. He knows that there is only one such place.

He glances up, their eyes meet. Fisher is looking over his glasses. Not even a clear lens separates the men. Fisher is right. He sees everything.

Just then a thought pulls Tom back. Over and over again it repeats itself and the idea emboldens him. "There has to be another way." Tom straightens up and so aggressively leans forward that Fisher is caught off guard, is now the one backing away.

"Sounds like you're going to arrest me."

Fisher recovers, leans into Tom. This time Tom holds his ground. "No. There'll be no arrests today. Like I told you earlier, you're free to go, but I've got to warn you that this investigation isn't done and I'm not going away. We will hold someone responsible."

Tom is surprised by his own moxie. He stands up, stands over Fisher.

"I hope you find your man."

Suddenly there is a clarity, the likes of which Tom has never known. He sees things as they will be. He sees tomorrow. He sees a warrant. He sees an arrest. He sees a trial. He sees the Lake Pulaski Daily, the mug shot, the headline, the story that "continues on page five". He sees *his* shame destroying Annie, disgracing Sophie, soiling the family name. It is all crystal clear. He needs time, more time.

    Staying ahead of the pack?

        Winning the race?

            There is always a way.

Always.

He is, after all, a Hyden.

Chapter 28

(The evening before the accident)

HIS PHONE VIBRATES, "RIBBET, RIBBET."

"I need to see you."

"What's up?"

"Something big...Can we talk?"

"Sure. Where?"

"Someplace private. Can't be overheard..."

Even though it's not the weekend, "someplace private" means that Sparky's, the coffee shop, or any of their usual meeting spots will not work.

"Your place?"

"No. Can't talk here. How about the city square? Let's take a walk..."

Early on they had agreed that they'd never be together alone. Even morning coffee in Kelly's kitchen happened before school, before the boys left home.

Joe offers no response.

"Please! I wouldn't ask if it wasn't important."

"Okay."

They meet. There are no pleasantries. Kelly is frantic and like a falling tree the story crashes around her. Her sentences are scattered, fragmented. Joe extends a hand, lets it rest on Kelly's shoulder. "Wait. Slow down Kelly. Take a minute."

Kelly pauses and gathers herself. "This afternoon Pete came home, mad as hell. He wouldn't say what, but something's screwed up with the bank. Whatever it is, he took it out on the boys and me. You know how he is, always a jerk, right? But this. I've never seen anything like it. Joe, he *hit* Frankie and threatened me. The boys were in the living room wrestling around, you've seen it. It isn't ever anything bad. It's just what they always do. Well Pete separated them, took Frankie by the arm and walloped him so hard that it left a welt on his, butt. I tried to stop him, but I couldn't. He shouted me down, called me a bitch, told me that if I didn't mind my own business, I'd be next." Kelly pauses. Her eyes are distant and fixed, as if she's reliving every word, every blow. She is shaking, literally shaking.

"This is it! I was going to stick it out, wait at least until the boys got a little older, but I can't. He's crossed the line. It's gotten so I don't feel safe. I am leaving him, Joe. I'm taking the twins and getting the hell out of here. I'm...I..."

Kelly is shaking. Joe stops her. "Kelly, it's the right thing. If he's pulling this crap, you *need* to get away from him. You need to go someplace else, someplace where you can start over."

"Joe, you don't understand." Kelly pauses. "OK, I'm just going to say it. I want to be with you. I love you. I want to take you with us. I don't care where it is, just so long as it's someplace far away. We'll go where you can set up your business." She pauses again, speaks slowly, earnestly. "I've spent a lifetime living with everything and having nothing, being Pete's Barbie doll and pretending I'm happy. I'm ready to live a different life, and even if that means I *have* nothing at least I'll *be* someone. I'll do anything to have you." She lifts a smile, makes a joke. "I'll drink bad coffee. I'll eat canned tuna. I'll live in a tent. I don't care. For the first time in my life, someone has made me feel like a real person and I don't want that to ever stop. You have done this Joe. You have changed my life. Come with me, Joe. I want *you*. I love you..."

"I love you...I want to be with you." This should be a bombshell, but isn't. Instead the words echo, then fill Joe's hollow heart.

Then suddenly the world flips, turns upside down.

"Kelly I...I can't."

"Joe, you've said it yourself. Your marriage is over. You didn't leave Jen, she left you. She chose a way that was not your way. She crawled into that bottle and didn't come out. You've tried. God knows you've tried! You've done your best, stuck by her, loved her, held onto her when anyone else would have been long gone. Joe, you know that you can't save her. You've said so yourself. How long's it been? Two, three years? You've given up everything and she continues to walk away."

Joe turns aside, but Kelly blocks his path. "Joe," She takes his hand, "you have been so alone. It's time for you to be happy again. I can give you that. We can give you that."

He looks down, squeezes her hand. The skin over her thumb is soft, warm, and it occurs to him that it has been years since anything has felt this real. He does not pull away. A wave like sensation gently rises, bringing a lightness that lifts him. Then, in the way of waves, it falls, darkens. "Happiness." He wonders what that means. Right now he hasn't a clue.

"Meet me tomorrow night. We'll start with a few days away...

drop the boys at my mom's and go somewhere warm, maybe even someplace where you can teach me to dive. We'll take some time, talk about the next step. Then we'll find a place far away and start a new life." Kelly's tone darkens, becomes gray, but also carries a genuineness, a resolve. "I want you with me, but this is not on you. Pete has crossed the line. With you or without you I am getting out. I am leaving and not coming back. Come with me, Joe. Please... come with me."

Again Kelly draws close. Again Joe does not pull away. Instead he feels himself leaning, falling. "Being wanted?" he thinks, "It feels so good." They kiss. He sees Jen. He sees her hurt, her pain. An odd mix, guilt, happiness, resentment, contentment, love, faithfulness, betrayal, it overwhelms him.

"Being wanted? It feels good." Again they kiss. He sees Joey and the void his death still creates. He sees the father he lost, the father he never became, and the love of his life who dumped him for her Novacaine. He thinks of the many ways he wanted to share the load, Jen's load and his, and he wonders why this empty burden has always been his responsibility, his only. Not once has Jen offered to hold his broken heart, or carry his mourning, or touch his hurting soul. Not once. Grief gone to seed, it is a selfish business. It soured Jen, turned her inward, isolated her heart, and built around her an impenetrable fence. Joe sees this and wonders if grief has finally done the same to him.

"Being wanted. It feels so good." The kiss becomes passionate. "It is so wrong." He wants to stop. He wants to push Kelly away, tell her no. He wants to jump in his truck, speed home, kick Jen in the ass. He is falling and he doesn't know how to stop it. The hole into which he tumbles corkscrews downward, becoming a black, murky pith. He wants to go with Kelly. Will he? He can't, he won't go with Kelly. He wants to lose everything he is. He is afraid that he will lose everything he is. He tries to hold these opposites together, but can't. They refuse to exist in the same space or live in the same heart.

Joe thinks about the local pilot who last summer planted his single engine Cessna into a corn field. That evening a dense cloud cover blanketed the earth so that when the pilot flew into the clouds, the horizon disappeared completely. While enveloped and flying blind something happened, something the pilot couldn't see, hear, or in any way sense. When he emerged, he thought he'd broken through and was now flying above the cover, but had, in fact, turned his plane upside down. A minute later he was dead.

Pilots call it vertigo, but to Joe this seems like the wrong word. To Joe, vertigo means dizzy, and while dizzy is uncomfortable, it is also recognizable and relatively safe. To Joe, vertigo is obvious and simple. The world is spinning. You know it is spinning. You lie down and wait. Eventually, the spinning stops and while your stomach might be upset, that's the end of it. When however pilots describe vertigo, they're describing something deceptively sensationless. It is more a disorientation of which pilot and passengers are completely unaware. That night, the pilot pulled his plane above the clouds, but he was really beneath them. He looked up which was down. Above him, he saw what he took to be stars, but were in fact street lamps and porch lights. He felt gravity pushing him into his seat. It wasn't gravity. It was an artificial g-force, created by the motion of his airplane as it plunged earthward. To counter his disorientation, that pilot had only a few lit dials, instruments telling him that the airplane was upside down and that he was about to die. He looked at those dials and probably thought to himself, "Damned things must be malfunctioning. Everything feels so right…"

Kelly. Her declaration of love, her willingness to share her life, her offer, it all feels so right.

A marriage license, Jen and her distance, her apathy, their non-relationship held together by a decades old vow, the nagging suspicion that easy is not real and real is not easy, it's just a few lit dials.

Is up down?

Are those the stars of the sky?

Is that the sky?

This is where Joe finds himself.

"Come with me, Joe."

"Kelly, I...uuuh...I don't know." This is all Joe can manage.

They agree that they will talk again tomorrow. Joe gets behind the wheel and drives. The night into which he travels is perfectly black. The trees, farm houses, earth, sky have all disappeared. The only thing he can see is darkness, and the hole his headlights carve in it. Of course, the hole is only so big. He wishes he could see more. He wishes that light would shine into tomorrow, next Wednesday, next year. It doesn't. It occurs to him that maybe everything beyond the hole is emptiness, a corkscrew spinning into nothing. It's not enough. Is he driving toward Kelly, away from Jen, or is he going someplace else? He does not know. He lets the truck make decisions. Into the hole it races. Joe hopes that some landmark will appear, a no passing sign, a mile marker, anything, but black becomes black becomes black. Beyond his headlights, there is nothing. Joe squeezes the gas pedal until he presses it against the floorboard. Into his seat, the motion pushes him. The highway and its center lines become a blur. Is he falling? He isn't sure. All he knows for certain is that he is now faced with the possibility that there may be only one way out, only one way to end the falling, and remove the hurt, and stop the pain that he is causing the people he loves.

Is he driving?
    Is he flying?
        Is he falling?
            He doesn't know.
Black turns to black.
    The hole narrows, shortens.
He can't find the light.

Chapter 29

Chec.
    Chec.
        Chec.
            Chec.

ON HIS BACK, TOM LAYS hearing, but not seeing the wall clock. Clouds break. A full moon shines and filters through the south window. Into the bedroom carpet it carves a bright rhombus. The light scatters, casts dull shadows, etches outlines, the dresser, night stand, lamp.

    He tries closing his eyes. He can't. He watches the ceiling fan spin and how, with a strobe like precision, the blades catch the moon's reflection. He hears the clock. Save a gentle rise and fall, Annie's slumber, there are no other sounds, no breeze pushing against the window, no dogs barking, no cars moving, just the damned clock. It fills the night. Exact. Measured. Time is sliced, creating tiny, empty cubes, each one perfect as the next. The checs seem to get louder, but that can't be. They're all the same. He knows that. He wonders if maybe it's the stacking. One hollow box clicking on the next, the echo of each resonating against the others. All the while each stacked cube adds a little height, a little volume, a little weight so that time becomes an unstable tower, perfect blocks teetering to and fro. Of course during the day, when the tower rests upon his shoulders, it is manageable, a matter of balance, but laying here like this, when the thing shifts from his shoulders to his chest, it gets so he can hardly catch a breath.

That "prestigious" last name.

The portraits on the bank wall and the one that's missing.

The expectations he'd never meet.

His father. Oh, his father...

Cube after cube,

so many cubes that he knows he'll never fill.

Weight.

Pressure.

Life is a balancing act and until now he's always found a way, but this, this one last cube. It seems so much larger than the others.

"Time." He mouths the word. "Why do we do this crap? ...start with a perfectly good idea, something you can't quite get your head around and carve it down to size. Lifetimes, decades, years, days, weeks, hours, minutes, seconds. Slice it up. Make it look manageable. Create empty boxes, an endless supply of them, into which we organize all of life's little pieces, set them neatly upon the shelf, and pretend we're in control. After all, what else could time possibly be? I've got a cube for all the people I need to see or maybe ignore. I've got cubes for Annie and Sophie, work and next month's vacation. I've got Rotary on Wednesday, church on Sunday, and, thanks to a little ingenuity, a stack of bills I can now pay on or before the 15th. Get angry? Put it on the to-do list where maybe it will cool, become nothing. Fix Annie's bruised ego? Schedule it for a week from Tuesday, set it right on top of last Friday's fight and my never-spoken resentments. There isn't a thing in the world that once on the shelf, won't lose urgency. Love. Hate. Regret. Remorse. Meeting everyone's damned expectations, just schedule it, postpone it and with any luck bury it. So I check the calendar, fill my little boxes, but they're all still empty. I neatly stack my crap, pat myself on the back for my ingenuity, and lose half my stomach making sure the teetering tower never falls. Tick toc, tick toc. It's so unnatural and so flippin' typical. What a stupid little world!

"Sometimes I wonder, what the hell's wrong with 'stop the car, I gotta pee' or 'screw the deadline, there's a spectacular sunset that's about to disappear!' What's wrong with time as it really is, an unruly giant, unsliced, unstacked, and defying our pathetic attempts to control it? Time maybe...like the sea...fluid, uncontainable, where if you tried to pick it up, it'd slip through your fingers. Time...deep past all reach and wide beyond human sight, with sweeping currents that carry me wherever it damned well pleases.

"Something like that'd scare the crap out of people. I mean really, who could live that way? So out come the carving knives. Cube it up. Tame it. Turn the wild coyote into a lap dog, or so everybody thinks. That's what we do."

He stops. Draws a deep breath. Releases it. "Still, sometimes I wonder... I've spent a lifetime stacking make believe cubes, creating illusions, and convincing myself that they're real. I've been swimming against those currents and I'm beat—might just feel good to go for a ride."

Annie adjusts her shoulders, rolls toward him, and resumes her quiet rise and fall. He turns toward her and gently, so that she'd not notice, brushes her bangs behind her ear. Her lips tense, turn upward just a bit, and then return.

Annie. In this light, her face is delicate, even more so than usual. She looks like a cut glass figurine,

    slender body and perfectly fixed features,

        facets catching sparse moonlight,

            fragile...so fragile...

Tom studies her and wonders, "How is it that she still casts that spell over me, still stops time..."

Fisher's chair. Being trapped. Exits disappeared. One last time, he weighs options, imagines waiting it out, but wonders if the silt would clear before his tank runs dry. Then he remembers the dive reel.

"Thank God for the dive reel. I need to go. I need to find clear water."

Early in his career, Jacques Cousteau discovered that deep water diving had an unexpected effect on the mind. At depths below 100 feet, he experienced a profound sense of euphoria which he called the Rapture of the Deep. The technical term for this experience is nitrogen narcosis and is a temporary condition that affects every diver differently. As a diver descends, the bloodstream absorbs nitrogen creating a state of mind mimicking the effects of alcohol. Symptoms include a feeling of tranquility, a god-like over-confidence, uncontrolled laughter, and loss of focus, delayed reaction time, hallucinations and tunnel vision. For some, the mood can swing quickly causing the diver to experience extreme anxiety, paranoia, and vertigo.

Since the diver's most important piece of safety equipment is his or her sense of judgment, nitrogen narcosis can be VERY dangerous. As we've stated elsewhere, panic or over-confidence can have lethal results. Cousteau assigns the condition a healthy respect when he says, "I am personally receptive to nitrogen rapture. I like it and fear it like doom. It destroys the instinct of life."

Open Water SCUBA Certification Manual
Compiled by DII (Dive Instructors International)
Pg. 79

Chapter 30

This morning two very odd things happen.

~~~~~~~~~~~~~~~~~~~~

Joe stops at the Gas Shack, fills his truck, grabs a cup of coffee and some breakfast pizza. Today, he's heading south, Des Moines, where he'll finish a remodel. This wasn't his plan, but lately plans haven't meant much. Right now? He needs windshield time. He needs space. He needs to do things that make sense. Jen. Kelly. Last night. The world is unhinged and there's nothing to do, but drive, nothing to do, but measure...

mark,
    tap,
        cut,
            study...

Des Moines is a two and a half hour drive. Once he arrives, he figures that the remaining job will take ten and a half, maybe eleven hours. He decides he will work into the night, find a cheap motel, and head back early tomorrow. He also knows that Annie and Tom need their space. For the last six days, the Hyden basement has been his home. "Damned nice of Annie, letting me use their guest room," he thinks, "especially under these circumstances, but I don't want to wear out the welcome."

In truth, this will be his second night out. Last night the truck was his home.

Driving.
    Thinking.
        More driving.

No sleep.

Tomorrow Joe will call a couple of Lake Pulaski landlords, schedule a few showings. He's hopeful that by the first of the week he can find his own apartment.

...Hopeful...Find his own apartment...It sounds so certain and so permanent. In truth, he doesn't really know what's next. The idea is as empty as he imagines the apartment will be that the landlord will show. This is all so strange and so completely unwanted.

He stands in line. Three guys are ahead of him, buying energy drinks, donuts, cigarettes. Between the two registers is the lottery kiosk. It's flashing an alert, "This Week's Jackpot? A Cool 118 Million Dollars." A ticket a week, just one...When they were first married this was Jen's only splurge. It became a running joke. She promised that *when* her number is called, she'd buy Joe a waterfront lot, a place where they could escape January's cold. Joe would build the house, while she'd sun herself and deliver the beer.

Everything reminds him of her.

His cell phone vibrates. It's Jen. He hits a button and sends the call to voice mail. Since he left, Jen calls several times a day. He has yet to answer. He doesn't intend cruelty, he just doesn't know what he would say. Every time he hears her voice, the tsunami rushes him. Every time the phone chirps, he feels the resentment rise, the two years of rejection, the apathy, the bitterness, the lovelessness–they flood him. He can't face it. Maybe sometime he will answer, again hear her voice, but not now. Not yet. The phone vibrates. Joe just lets it ring. It's easier.

He steps up to the register, digs in his pocket, and finds his wallet. His credit card is gone. Did he leave it on the dresser? He's not sure, so he reaches inside the wallet and grabs one of the twenties he knows is there. It's not a twenty, it's a one hundred. He pulls the folds apart and finds 15 such bills, neat, crisp, upright, all facing the same direction.

~~~~~~~~~~~~~~

About an hour after Joe makes his discovery, Annie's alarm chirps. She rolls out of bed and walks down the hallway. Soon, the TV is glowing and the tea kettle rattling. As she loads the coffee grinder, she notices last night's empty wine bottle sitting beside the toaster. It is odd, because she distinctly remembers tossing the bottle into the recycling bin. She looks more closely. A piece of cream colored paper is rolled up and pushed into the neck, a half an inch of which rides above the opening. She smiles. "He's so whipped," She whispers. Last night was good. It has been weeks since they'd connected like this, weeks since he'd shown his usual tenderness, his romantic playfulness. Inside the bottle she slips a finger, retrieves the note, unrolls it. Across the top of the memo sized paper, the words *Lakeland Savings and Trust* are printed. Just beneath this and in Tom's meticulous cursive, she sees the words, "It is an accident..." In the bottom right hand corner a smiley face winks at her.

Annie studies the note and wonders what it means.

Chapter 31

The water is cool.
    And blue.
        Deep.
            Penetrating.
                Perfectly clear.

I AM SUSPENDED—NOT SUSPENDED AS though caught between two places and not suspended, like I'm dangling, waiting as a frayed rope finally breaks and gravity fulfills its legal duties. No. This suspension is more like abeyance, like universal forces are laid aside. Can it be? Is it possible? That which, by nature's design, would propel me into some irresistible center no longer applies. The world as I know it has come to an end, its native claims hushed, and I hang here, primal powers seeking, but not finding me. Freedom, pure, simple, yet impossible freedom, it surrounds me and inexplicably confers its perfect, intoxicating peace.

Above me, bleached ripples form a translucent ceiling, a barrier between worlds that always touch, but never meet. Blades of afternoon sun cut deep diagonals, illuminating tiny particles. In and out of those slices they drift.

    Appearing.

        Disappearing.

In front of me, pink fans sway, yellow branches randomly twist. Beneath a crimson ledge, a school of caesar grunts motionlessly hang. French angels, triggerfish, blue tangs glide. Around and under the folded labyrinth they appear, disappear. At the doorway of his home, a small spotted eel waits, opening and closing his mouth as though he is gasping for air.

Gasping for air... It's odd. Above the ceiling is all the air in the world and I cannot breathe there, but here? Here everything is so easy. Flick an ankle, flip a fin, even filling and emptying my lungs, such simple acts yet they all move me. Forward, backward, up, down. Unfettered, effortless I glide. It is all so easy.

Maybe the eel and I should trade places.

I check my gauges. I don't know what they say. I look again. "Air pressure?" "Check!" "Depth?" "Check!" I giggle because I still don't know what they say. I don't care. I giggle again, harder. Around my ears and above me bubbles curl then balloon. I don't care. It feels good.

    Hovering.

        Suspended.

            Weightless.

Finally, I'm weightless.

From somewhere beneath me I hear her voice. I know that voice. Who is it? I haven't a clue, but it is beautiful, inviting, soft.

"Thomas...

Thomas James.

    Come home, Thomas.

Come home..."

Below me the coral drops forming a vertical wall. It reaches straight down. How far? Who the hell knows? The color deepens until blue becomes unearthliness and unearthliness becomes nothing.

"Come home, Thomas.

    Come home..."

I glance over and see my dive partner. Is it Annie? I can't say. I raise my eyebrows. With two fingers, I touch the side of my mask and flip them toward her, a cub scout salute. "You're on your own, sweetheart." The words roll around my neck, float to the surface. I shoot my partner one more glance,

    "Hear that voice?

        "I need to go find her.

        "She knows the way home."

Toward the sound of her voice I fin. As I do, I realize that we *have* met before. So many times she has called my name. Lying in bed. Watching the clock. Why did I wait this long? I don't know, but I have to wonder why in the world would she want *me?* She is, after all, formed of formlessness, of such perfect immensity that one would expect indifference. Still she calls. Gently, longingly, as though I am her lost lover, she calls. And because she does I will follow that voice. I will find her.

As I do, I feel the last residuals, my life above the ceiling, peel away and begin their slow ascent,

    rising,

        to their native land rising.

I am naked.

~ David Grindberg ~

    Unashamed.
        Free.
"Come home Thomas.
    Come home..."
        I quicken my pace.
The water is cool.
    The blue deepens...
        and narrows...
            and wraps me in her endless embrace.

Chapter 32

Nothing.
    No light. No dark.
        No sound. No silence.
    Nothing.
        Time is suspended.
            Dreams are not remembered.

THE UNIVERSE COLLAPSES INTO ITSELF, and the space it occupies is so full that nothing enters. Nothing leaves. It is an impenetrable fog, formed yet formless, shell-like yet lacking discernable boundaries. It is an inviting womb cradling a mother's first love. This nothing cannot be achieved or possessed. Like gentle rain interrupting a mid-summer's drought, it simply happens and when it does, it brings with it perfect repose.

Such is her slumber, night's deepest and her first in weeks. Oh yes, she has tried. For days on end, she has tried. On her side, she has laid and watched as the clock dutifully checked away the minutes. She has poured up a Jack-n-Coke, and another, and another. She has even taken the doctor's pills, which provided sleep, but no rest. This evening is different. Tonight, the gift chooses her. Into a natal solitude it takes her, the ideal shelter from that which for so long has robbed her sleep.

The fog is in fact so deep that when the doorbell rings, it goes nearly unnoticed. It is just a faint echo. The second ring brings the dull awareness that something outside this womb is calling. She reaches over to nudge Joe and remembers that he isn't there. The idea jolts her. Some, but not all of the fog clears.

"He still has a key." Jen mutters. She pushes back the sheets, fumbles around, finds the lamp switch. She hopes it's him.

It's not.

Just beyond the threshold stand two men. Both are wearing dark blue, one chubby, the other tall. The tall one she thinks she recognizes. "Jennifer Johnson?" He asks. "Your husband is Joseph E. Johnson, right?" Jen nods. They introduce themselves. She doesn't hear their names. They produce their badges. She looks, but doesn't see.

They show Jen a fax. It is a copy of Joe's diver certification card. "Is this your husband?"

Jen glances at the paper. "Yes, of course it is...How did you get this? What's going on?"

"This evening we were contacted by the authorities in Mexico. They sent us this fax."

"Mexico?"

"Your husband is missing and is presumed dead..."

Jen stares vacantly. It is as if they've not spoken. She waits, wondering when they will say something.

"Mrs. Johnson? Would you like to sit down?"

She does not move. "Wh...What was that!?"

"Your husband is missing, ma'am."

They tell the story. "Apparently Mr. Johnson flew to Cozumel this morning."

"Cozumel?"

"He checked into his hotel and then booked a charter to go diving. The dive master said that he'd not met Mr. Johnson before, but he had this card with him. The dive master has confirmed that the picture on the card matched the man who is missing.

"...Cozumel?"

"At some point, Mr. Johnson evidently became disoriented and swam past safe limits. His dive partner saw what was happening. She tried to stop him, but could not. He just swam, deeper and deeper until he was out of sight. The dive master believes the disorientation was due to something called..," the officer unfolds a slip of paper and glances down, "nitrogen narcosis. The boat captain called the Mexican Coast Guard. Together they initiated a search which at sunset was suspended. While the coast guard promised they'd look for him again tomorrow, the place where he went missing is quite deep. They may never find him."

Jen hears nothing. She watches the officer's lips. They move, but there is no sound. Over her eyebrow, she runs three fingers. She feels nothing. Somewhere beneath her lungs, a single syllable rises and repeats itself, a whisper at first and the only thing Jen really hears. As it rises, it fills her lungs with the kind of urgency that comes as one's breath can no longer be held.

"no. no. No. No! NO! NNOOOH!"

She runs to the bedroom and finds her phone. She calls. He does not answer. She calls again. Again. Again. She hears his recorded greeting and shouts over the voice mail instructions. "Come home Joe! Damn you, come home! Come! Home!..."

She backs away, two or three half steps. Into a leather easy chair she falls, melts. As she does, that syllable, now mixed with muted sobs, recedes, returning to the place from where it first rose. "NO. No. no..."

"I'm so sorry Mrs. Johnson," the officer pauses, "We need to ask you a few questions. What can you tell us about your husband's trip?"

There is a long silence as she reads his lips and tries to form the words that were never meant to be spoken. "I...I didn't...didn't know he was going...anywhere. You see h...he left. About a week ago. He...He left me. We uh, we agreed to..." Jen hears her own voice trail away. Again she melts. Around her the leather folds. This time there is no return. Her mouth moves. There is no sound.

The tall one asks another question, but by now Jen cannot see his lips. The room with all its sound and silence, all its light and darkness explodes. The walls and ceiling peel themselves away exposing a black and expansive night. It is a blackness brimming with remorse and an expansiveness that cannot contain her guilt. Like the tip of a fountain pen pressed into a paper towel, it saturates the night and spreads its inky hues. Jen's hands, her hair, the chair, the officers, and the threshold, and the squad parked in the driveway, and the cloud covered dome above her, everything large, everything small is stained. Toward her, away from her it seeps until every corner, every edge, every crack fills, and beneath it all the single syllable whispers its futility.

"no. no. no..."

Chapter 33

DOWN THE RAMP, JOE'S PICKUP first coasts then accelerates. He has just finished a pit stop and now merges back onto the interstate. In another 30 minutes he will be home. The cell phone rings. It's Annie. He finds this curious. She never calls.

"Hey Annie. What's up?"

There's a pause. "Joe?" It's Jen's voice. Joe is confused, takes the phone from his ear, checks the display. This is definitely Annie's phone number.

"Joe? Joe??! It's Joe!!!" Now Jen is shouting. "He's on the phone! It's Joe!!! He's not dead! He's not dead!"

"Jen, what the hell are you talking about, and why are you on Annie's phone?"

"He's not dead!!!"

"Slow down, babe. Talk to *me.* Tell me what's going on here."

"The cops came last night, told me you went to Mexico, that you got yourself killed diving. I'm talking to Joe! *He's not dead!*"

Joe is about to reply when he hears something that, in nearly two years, he's not heard.

"You stupid jerk! I called you fifteen times last night. Why the hell didn't you answer me?" The fire in her voice is so hot that instinctively he peels the phone off his ear. "I don't care if you are leaving me, when I call at one in the morning, you damned well better answer!!!"

Just then, Joe remembers his wallet, the missing credit card, the upright hundreds. A thought shadows him, a thought so dark that before he can form the words, he needs to pause.

"Has anyone called Tom?"

"Don't change the subject on me, you moron!" Jen is shouting, "Why the hell didn't you pick up last night?"

Joe pauses, leaving a silence that, for him, fills a short space of forever. "Jen you can have my hide later, this *is important.*" Very slowly he repeats the words. "Has anyone called Tom?"

Jen so knows Joe and his quiet urgency, that this short space and its forever, now finds her. "No... No, Annie can't reach him. He's in Minneapolis...some kind of banker's meeting." She pauses. "Joe? What's going on?"

"I don't know? Are you with Annie?"

"Yeah."

"Stay with her. Don't say anything. I'll be there in fifteen."

Joe tosses the phone. It hits the passenger seat, bounces, lands on the floorboard. Joe doesn't notice. He squeezes the gas pedal.

Chapter 34

Sorting things out takes a while. Joe makes phone calls, first to Tom, who does not answer, then to the same officer who just last night knocked on Jen's door and announced his demise. Next Joe goes online and finds yesterday's credit card purchases, $1,132.50. $215.20. $110.00, an airline ticket, a room at the Laguna Azul, a two tank boat dive. Again he calls Tom...leaves a message. Then he contacts the hotel, the dive shop, and the Minneapolis International Airport Parking Security.

The pieces begin to fit.

Security locates Tom's car. The dive shop has Joe's scuba certification and credit card. The hotel manager opens the room and over the phone describes its contents, an airline ticket, a passport belonging to Joseph Johnson, a change of clothes, and a wallet containing only two pictures, one of an attractive woman, her thick hair pulled into a pony tail, and the other of a young girl wearing red leotards with silver sequins.

Then Joe calls Mary Wilke, Tom's assistant.

"Business trip?" At first, Mary sounds confused. "There was no business trip. No. Yesterday Tom called in sick, said he'd be gone the rest of the week." There is a long silence. Mary begins to cry.

"What's going on?"

Mary can't answer.

"Mary?"

"You don't know where he is?" Her voice becomes urgent. "Annie? She doesn't know where he is?"

"No...Mary tell me what's going on here!"

"I think Tom...Mr. Hyden...I think he is in some kind of trouble..."

"What do you mean?"

"I don't know for sure. Somebody from the state has been talking to him. I...I'm afraid for him."

Joe hangs up.

"What did she say," Annie asks.

"There were no meetings. He called in sick." Joe doesn't tell her the rest.

~~~~~~

Word of Tom's disappearance spreads. Dori and Meg arrive first. They hug Annie and offer their help.

Meg makes coffee, sets out dishes, napkins, and silverware. Dori tends the front door and receives the neighbor's offerings; fruit trays, cakes, casseroles, pies. The kitchen island soon becomes a buffet.

It isn't long before others come knocking. Most of the visitors simply hand Dori their gifts and leave. A few of Annie's closer friends stay, drink coffee, take turns sitting with Annie, stand around the island and graze. Annie responds exactly as she should. She smiles when she should, cries when she should, receives sympathies when she should. She doesn't know what else she could do. It is all so surreal. Somewhere in the back of her mind, something tells her that this is a gigantic mistake and at any moment Tom will pop through the door, offer some perfectly logical explanation, and everyone will go home.

Joe keeps busy. The police come and he answers their questions. He again calls Mexico. This time he speaks directly with the dive master. The man's voice is tense, nervous sounding, like he's afraid of the police, the coast guard, something. Joe asks about the I.D. Now the man is not at all sure if the photo *was* an exact match. Did he tell the authorities what he thought they wanted to hear? Was he protecting himself? Joe can't say. He asks more questions. Tom was diving Maracaibo, a wall that begins at ninety feet and bottoms out somewhere around fifteen hundred[4]. Joe knows the dive and its swift current. While this is considered an advanced dive (over 130 feet deep) requiring advanced equipment, it is certainly within Tom's skill level.

Joe makes more phone calls, gathers information, and keeps Annie updated. Every so often, he glances over and tries catching Jen's eye. The two of them have not yet spoken, and Jen does not return the attempt. For her part, she waits until he turns away, then watches him, studies him.

---

4. Recreational divers limit themselves to depths no greater than 130 feet. Anything beyond 130 feet requires advance training

~ David Grindberg ~

Death has its own time, an insistent rhythm that trumps everything else. It halts routines, cancels appointments, suspends conversations and appetites. That which, before death, looked important is properly sized, and all of life's self-evident purposes are hung with question marks. After all, what does one do when there's nothing that can be done? What does one say about something that stops the world cold? Do you go about your usual business, work, make money, pay the bills, fund retirements? Do you hit Sparky's, grab a beer, meet some friends? Do you come home, ignore your kids, watch television while your wife tries to tell you about her day? Last week, next week, last night, this morning, pressing matters and ordinary things become what they really are and everyone finds themselves asking the same question. "What the hell went wrong?"

This is death's time and it shakes everyone. Its rhythm has us re-evaluating the life we think we know.

Jeff walks through the living room, finds Meg. The two of them slip back into the pantry, slide the pocket door closed, hold hands. Jeff whispers long unspoken affections. It creates a thawing. Iciness melts. Old, comfortable shirts are removed, laid aside.

Pete stops, finds Annie. They hold each other. He has a full morning, four appointments and a lunch meeting. He looks lost. He stays.

Dori opens the door, receives more casseroles.

Aggie calls. Frank cannot travel. Pete talks to her, then to him. His voice is tender, soft. His words kind.

Time stretches.

Spaces open.

    Death's rhythm first disrupts then becomes its own gift, and out of the chaos, new things form.

Jen, who just hours ago lost everything, now finds that she is drawn to Sophie. Why exactly, she can't say. She knows that Sophie needs her, but it is more than that. Unlike Annie, Sophie is completely transparent. She is lost, alone, desperately needing, and even if Sophie wanted, she couldn't hide this. Jen stays beside her. The two of them play board games, read books, watch television. Mostly though, Sophie asks questions, questions that Jen can't answer. She doesn't try. She looks into Sophie's eyes and in them Jen sees her own pain, her own unanswered questions. For years, Jen has avoided these things, soaked them in alcohol and covered them beneath her carefully constructed indifference. That protective shell had become so well-crafted and so comfortable that she had almost forgotten how much she really hurts. Now here she is, immersed in Sophie's raw vulnerability and it threatens to rip open her own wounds. Yet something odd is happening. She knows she should be afraid, but she is not. Instinct tells her that she should find Jack, but she doesn't. In that moment, with this hurting lost child, something changes, flips her world upside down. That which for so long rendered her life pointless now twists with purpose. She slips an arm around Sophie and Sophie holds her. With all her life, she holds her.

"He didn't come up. Jen, he said he'd always come up. He didn't come up."

"I know, sweet girl. I know." Jen cradles her, rocks her, and in a tone so soft that only Sophie can hear, she hums Joey's lullabies.

    Gently,

        tenderly,

            Jen hums.

Dr. Lisa says, "When pillars all around you fall, you alone can stand tall."

Dori finds Annie. "There's someone here to see you—some state investigator. If you want, I'll ask him to come back another time."

"No, he might have some answers. I'd like to see him."

Dori leaves, returns, introduces Dennis Fisher. Until this moment, Annie has never met him, never even heard his name.

"I'm sorry Mrs. Hyden. I know that this is a difficult time, but I need to ask a few questions."

"It's ok." Into Tom's study Annie leads Fisher and closes the door so that it is open just a crack. "Tom told me he had banker's meetings. Evidently he didn't. Evidently he went..." Annie pauses, gathers herself. "I'm sorry. I wish I understood this."

"I'm so sorry Mrs. Hyden." Fisher pauses, finds Annie's eyes. "For the last several weeks, I've been conducting an investigation. Someone has been embezzling from the bank, and we believe that your husband was involved."

"What?"

"I'm sorry, ma'am."

"No." Annie is matter of fact, "No, not Tom. He'd never do anything like that. Tom's a good man. That...that can't be true!"

"I'm afraid it is, and we have a mountain of proof. Two days ago, I showed Mr. Hyden the evidence and asked him to tell me the truth. He ended the conversation abruptly and when he left, he knew that we would soon issue a warrant."

"How much money was taken?"

"Just a little over $87,000." Fisher pauses again. "I know this is difficult to hear. I believe your husband took Mr. Johnson's identity so that he could leave the country undetected. Did he ever mention any of this to you?"

Annie shakes her head.

"When you last saw him, did he act odd, say anything about leaving?"

Something in Annie rises. What is it? She can't say exactly. It rises. She straightens her back.

"My husband didn't steal money. That bank means everything to him. It is a family business, his *father's* bank. Tom couldn't...He is incapable of such things...and if you think he'd run from trouble, or that he would kill himself over a piddly $87,000, you're wrong. It is an accident."

She rubs a hand over her pocket. The note is neat, folded, its outline nearly invisible. Like lead, it sits there. For the first time, she feels its full weight. In her ear, it whispers. She alone hears its cryptic voice. While Annie has always been self-sufficient, this is different. She glances around and takes stock of the palace they've built. Now all of it, the decor, the design, the windows and their coverings, the hardwood floors, cherry cabinets, and granite counter tops breaks up, becomes rubble heavy with their secrets. Beneath it she is buried, and never has she been this alone, this isolated.

She pauses, slowly repeats the words, "It is an accident."

"Yes ma'am."

"So what's next?" Annie takes full command. "Are you going to investigate me?"

"No ma'am, we have no reason to believe that you are involved, and since we now have no suspect, the matter is closed. The bank has insurance for such things. Everyone will be repaid." Fisher stands up, extends a hand, which Annie receives. While there is a physical distance between them, Fisher's farewell is as much an embrace as it is a hand shake. "I'm sorry about your husband's death. I'm sorry for you and your little girl. I have reason to believe that he loved you very much."

"Thank you officer."

Fisher leaves and Annie can't breathe.

She carries her secret. Through the great room, kitchen, hallway, and the sea of faces she quietly weaves. Dori makes eye contact, places a hand on Annie's shoulder, gently squeezes. Annie nods her appreciation, lowers her eyes. Down the hallway and into her bedroom, she keeps moving. She closes and locks the door. She goes further, into the en suite. She closes and locks the door. She stops the drains, all of them, opens the faucets, all of them. The shower runs. The tub, the sinks fill. Steam rises.

Everything looks purposeful, but, in fact, Annie has no idea what she is doing or why she is doing it. She is numb, completely numb.

Piece by piece, she removes her clothing, sweater, bra, socks, slacks, panties. She straightens each item, finds the crease, folds and stacks them. The note is still in the pocket. She leaves it there. She lays the stack aside. By now the windows, mirrors, chrome fixtures, shower door, even the tumbler that sits beside the sink are fogged. She looks through the window, but there is no seeing in and no seeing out. She turns toward the mirror, but recognizes only shadows, only border-less outlines, only things that might be. She wipes a hand across the mirror. A stranger appears, her mascara smudged, her eyes vacant, lost. Annie wonders, "Is this a real person?" She isn't sure.

The faucets run. The steam rises. Into the fog, the stranger disappears.

Annie lies in the tub. Warm, embryonic water covers her. She sinks. Further she sinks, until only her lips and nose remain unsubmerged. She closes her eyes, feels the darkness swaddle her. She listens, hears only her own, steady breathing.

Inhale.

Exhale.

Her torso rises, falls.

Another.

Another.

Beneath the water's surface her breathing is amplified and becomes the only sound in an otherwise empty universe. Air leaves her lungs. The warm water floods over her sinking chest until she is completely submerged.

She waits, holds her breath.

She wants never again to draw another.

Chapter 35

THE LAST OF THE VISITORS leave. Meg and Dori finish the dishes. Sophie is spending the night with Jen. Annie must be asleep. It's been a while since anyone's seen her.

"Ribbit, ribbit." Joe doesn't check.

He closes the guestroom door and flops onto the bed. It catches him, cushions the fall, cradles him. He knows he should cry, but can't. Right now, there is a calm, and while he cannot tell if it's a real calm or the product of fatigue, this momentary solace opens and he welcomes it. The space it creates looks familiar, as familiar as the rolling farmland between Lake Pulaski and Des Moines. There is, however, one difference. The space has no interstates, no highways, no county roads, no gravel, a fact that so heightens the space's calming effect that without hesitation he enters it. In a random, pattern-less fashion he wanders. He sees his life. His back yard, the fallen ash, his father's face and the way it fills the night.

He sees Jen at bat, Jen rocking Joey, Jen inside her shell. Jen.

Then Joe sees Eldo and the trailer. "A spoon." He mouths the words. "A damned spoon." Their friendship spanned a lifetime and only once did Joe's anger turn itself toward Tom. They'd barely broken the surface and Joe spit the regulator from his mouth, "What the hell are you thinking." He hissed the words. "You idiot! What am I supposed to tell Annie, that you made her a widow chasing a piece of stainless steel?"

Joe lies across the bed, again sees it happen. The dive, the trailer, the door, the unearthly calm, the unknown reflection, the thick brown silt, suddenly it all makes perfect sense. Shiny promises mess with your mind. They lead you into a world where illusions become reality, a world so seductive that you'd risk everything just to make it your own. Up on the surface, the smallest of things are so damned difficult, but down deep? Down in that dark water... not only does nothing look like everything, but it presents itself as the lowest of low hanging fruit. Abandon all caution? Cross that threshold? Forget the hidden dangers? Chase everything? It makes perfect sense.

Joe looks at his phone. The red light flashes. The screen is dark, like a black hole. It invites him into its event horizon, into the point of no return. He imagines how that might be, starting over, no history, no messiness, never going back to a place where you have to face who you really are. How could it get any easier?

He looks again. The red light still flashes. It all makes perfect sense.

Then Joe sees Jen. For good or ill, his life is tied to her and anything else with anyone else is just a shiny something, just a trap waiting to be sprung, just a lie. He imagines the future, lets a divorce unfold all the while relying on the contingency called Kelly, but this too is a betrayal. It is a biding of time, playing all the cards in all the right order and knowing the outcome before it happens.

He unlocks his phone, erases the pending messages, blocks her number. "Not yet. Not now. Not ever. This is the way it has to be." Long ago, he made a promise and if Jen can't reciprocate, if she won't, Joe knows that it's the smallest most difficult things that also make him what he is. He is Jen's husband and even through a divorce, he must be true to first things. Without this, his life is a sham.

It hurts. Jen hurts. Kelly hurts. He hurts. He hurts in more ways than he can count, but he must be who he is.

Chapter 36

Joe knocks, tries the door. It is unlocked. He steps inside. Nothing has changed. The grandfather clock, the crowbar, the table over which they last spoke, Jack and his empty glass, everything is as it always is.

"Jen?...Sophie?..." No one answers. "Anybody here?"

He hears something, turns, looks up. Jen is standing in the kitchen doorway. He doesn't know how long she's been there. She says nothing.

"I...I'm here for Sophie. Thought I'd get her back to Annie."

"She's already gone. Meg picked her up a half an hour ago."

Joe nods, doesn't move. He is, in fact, frozen, unable to move. Jen straightens herself, shifts her weight, tilts her head slightly. The room is thick with expectation. They face each other, waiting, looking, but not speaking.

"Well?" Jen breaks the silence first.

"Well what?"

"Sweet mother of God. 1 a.m. 15 frantic phone calls. I lose my mind thinking you're dead, and all you can say is 'Well What!'?"

Joe has a thousand things he wants to say. He wants to apologize for this, for everything. He wants to tell her about last night, show her his cell phone and what he has done. He wants to ask for a fresh start, tell her how much he loves her, hold her, work things out, but her caustic challenge triggers something. Right now, all he can see is the swing of a bat and a wiry tom boy walking bases. Right now all he can see is a baseball sailing over his head. He watches its graceful rise, its arch, its descent. Smaller, smaller it becomes until somewhere at the playground's far end a white dot ricochets against the monkey bars and beside the chain link fence finds its rest.

Instinct takes over, leaving only one choice. "If you weren't such a pain in the ass, maybe I'd pick up once in a while."

Jen's eyes flame. She turns, disappears. Joe follows her.

"Wait a minute". Joe puts a hand on Jen's shoulder and turns her. They are eyeball to eyeball. "You think you're the only one hurting here? I've got news for you, princess. You're not! I miss him too, but you've been so pig headed that you think you're the only thing on the face of the planet, that you're the only one who matters and everyone else can go to hell! You and that stinking bottle of yours. You had a friend in me! Why did you have to go there, you selfish..."

"...At least with the bottle, I knew what I was going to get." Jen interrupted, "I knew it wasn't going to give me this crap. But you! How the hell am I supposed to know that you're hurting, you sorry, stone faced idiot? Living with you is like living with the statues on Easter Island...and reading you is like trying to get the time from a clock with no numbers and no hands. Why didn't you tell me this stuff? Let me in? You always act like nothing ever matters. What the hell am I supposed to think? And then, just when I'm starting to feel better, you head off with coffee girl."

Joe opens his mouth to defend himself, but the nothing that comes out leaves her last words, "coffee girl" hanging.

At the top of her voice, Jen shouts "I hate..." She hesitates.

"Say it, Jen."

"Ooooh!..."

"Say it! Damned you, say it!!!"

"I hate you, you son of a bitch!"

The words thunder then echo, and the ensuing silence stops everything. It stops Jen. It stops Joe. It stops the fight. Like molasses, it is thick, sticky and in it everything is mired, halted, suspended.

Joe hears a heaving, nearly inaudible yet heavy. Jen quietly sobs.

"No Joe. No.

   "I didn't...

      "I don't...

"I hate this.

   "I hate me.

      "I hate what I've become."

Until this moment, Joe doesn't realize it, but the two of them are close, so close they are nearly touching. The last crusty layer peels away and Jen melts. Joe melts. Into each other, they melt.

"Oh Joe.

   "It hurts, Joe.

      "It hurts so much..."

"I know Jen.

   "Let it go, babe.

      "Let it all go."

Twisters come.
    Homes destroyed.
        On their side, stately giants lay,
            leaving the world harshly exposed,
              baking,
                    beneath a blistering afternoon sun, baking.
Branches, limbs, slices of trunk.
    the wreckage of a life that once was, now lay fallen,
        exposing both its own deep wounds, and a road map,
           ring after ring,
                wide, narrow,
                    light, dark,
        and beautiful, oh so beautiful.
It spirals.
    Into its lovely darkness it spins.

How long has it been? Forever Joe thinks. In that forever, all he could find was bark's crusty, lifeless layers, one after the next, protecting something so deeply buried that he wondered if he'd ever again see it. Now, there it is once again, containing hundreds, no thousands of circles that together form the most beautifully rich pattern he has ever seen.

    "Let it go, Babe.
        "Let it all go..."

Chapter 37

THE MIRROR IS LIT, BUT not harsh, small, just 10 inches in diameter, but functional. A retractable arm holds it. Away from the wall, above the vanity, the mirror is suspended. In midair it hangs, looking like a magic window, a portal linking two worlds. Annie adjusts the arm, leans toward the light and in a slow, circular motion, moves her head. Right, left, up, down, carefully she examines that other world. An eye, an ear, a pair of lips, the 3x magnification slightly distorts everything and brings into plain view even the smallest imperfection.

She checks the time. 8:34 a.m. An 11:00 funeral means that she should be at the church by 10:15, no later. She opens her makeup drawer, sets out bottles, tubes, pencils, brushes and begins getting ready.

Three days ago, the Mexican authorities suspended their search and sent word that Tom's body may never be found. Annie wasted no time. Within two hours, she'd made arrangements, a day for notification, a day for the visitation, and now this morning the funeral. She wants this behind her.

Annie adjusts the portal, backing it away so that she can see its entire face.

Cream, base, powder.

After last night's visitation, Pete rang the doorbell. He came alone which was odd. Through all of this, Kelly has been conspicuously absent. Every Hyden woman knows that visibility is a non-negotiable expectation. Kelly never misses parties, social functions, and especially public family gatherings. Where has she been? All week Annie has wondered, but with so many people around, she couldn't inquire.

Pete apologized for the interruption and asked if he could have a few minutes. They sat down and he produced paperwork, the life insurance that was a part of Tom's executive benefits package. He explained the procedure, reviewed a few policy details, took a signature, and assured Annie that "you'll be comfortable for the rest of your life."

She leans forward. An eyebrow fills the window. Pluck, pencil.

"Comfortable..." That word spoken in this context sounded so very misplaced, a fact they both immediately recognized. The silence it created settled and in that space a question materialized, a question much larger than Kelly's whereabouts. Ever since Dennis Fisher dropped his little secret it has plagued Annie and she could no longer hold it inside.

"Pete, a few days ago this investigator guy came by, told me that Tom was in some trouble."

"Your husband left a hell of a mess." Pete's tone turned sour. His words rose then into nothing fell.

"Who knows about this?"

"Mary Wilke, the board of directors, you, and me. That's it and it needs to stay that way. I'm working with the board, identifying compromised accounts, rectifying the losses, and most of all putting into motion a damage control plan. Frankly, it's not the money so much as it is our reputation. This thing is a real powder keg. It's going to take some time, but with any luck we can keep it off the front page. If it stays low profile, I think we can save the family name."

Eyes. Shadow, liner.

She listened carefully and nodded her understanding. Annie's own reaction surprised her. This was the news she most dreaded, and she fully expected that Pete's confirmation would destroy her. It didn't. The revelation instead raised a second concern, "Who else knows?" She does not voice the question. Pete doesn't need to hear it.

Annie takes stock. She is nearly certain that Joe knows. It was after all his passport, his credit card. He made the phone calls that day, he gathered the information, and while Joe did not meet Dennis Fisher or hear the story, surely he must have put two and two together. Still, it isn't Joe that worries her. She wonders what if anything Dori, Meg, or anyone else may have overheard that day.

"What about Kelly?"

Pete shakes his head. "Kelly's gone."

Silence. Annie is left speechless, not that Kelly left, but that Pete would be so candid. She wants to say something, but doesn't know what it would be.

"...Been gone about a week." At first, his voice sounded empty, then angry, then something altogether different. Annie studied Pete's face and saw things she'd never before seen, eyes not alert, but distant, face not engaged, but expressionlessly withdrawn, voice not confident, but cracked. In all the years she's known him,

Annie has never seen him so utterly unguarded. The vulnerability is unhideable and makes Pete look like a complete stranger.

Lashes. Curl, mascara.

"Where'd she go?"

"Don't know for sure...came home from work and she and the boys were gone. They'd packed a couple suitcases and just left. Later that night she dropped me a text. I've tried tracking her, but then Tom pulled this little stunt... Pete stops, he'd forgotten to whom he was speaking. I'm sorry, Annie. I didn't..."

"It's ok, Pete. This thing's been tough on us all." Annie reaches over, places a hand upon his forearm. "I'm so sorry for you..."

Pete straightens up, his eyes focus, his voice firms, his game face returns. Instinctively Annie pulls back. Until this moment it had not occurred to her how much she and Pete have in common. She had always resented him and the way he rode Tom, but clearly her resentment clouded that which is now obvious. She plays along, redirects.

"How are your folks doing with this, Pete?"

"All they know is that Tom kil..."

Now it's Annie's turn. She raises her hand and, in mid-sentence, stops Pete.

"My husband didn't kill himself. It was an accident."

Their eyes meet. Pete nods.

Lips. Gloss, outline. Annie pauses, examines her work...

Even as a small child, Annie found her mother's morning ritual fascinating. The mirror, the bottles, the creams, the many tools and brushes, it wasn't just a task, it was an art and the finished product reminded Annie of the antique bisque doll that sat upon her bedroom shelf.

    Creamy colored porcelain skin, smooth, slightly translucent,
        delicate lips,

powdery pink cheeks,
> fine eyebrows,
>> subtly detailed lashes
>>> that accentuated bright hazel eyes,
in the space of 50 minutes, her mother,
> who even without the makeup
>> possessed a rare natural beauty,
> transformed herself,
became heavenly, Madonna-like.
a face set in perpetual bliss.

So each morning, Annie stood beside her mother and watched the master work. Then one day, it happened. How old was she? 13? Maybe a little younger? She isn't certain. All Annie knows is that one day she was given her own makeup kit. This wasn't the "Queen for a Day" play makeup. This was the real deal. As Annie applied the coats and colors, her mother watched, coached, "less is more." She said, "Enhance nature's gifts. *Subtly* cover the blemishes and imperfections."

"Soon it will be Sophie's turn." Annie sits back, smiles. The idea excites her. She will teach Sophie the way her mother taught her.

Cheeks. Blush.

One more time she adjusts the portal, first toward her and then away from her. She looks, sees a blemish, a smudge, a couple of needed touch-ups. Usually Annie finds this process energizing, but today, for some reason, she is tired.

"No makeup." She thinks. "Just once going with no makeup... how would that be?"

She imagines herself one morning rolling out of bed and leaving the house as she is;
no hair spray,
> no base,

>no blush,
>>or eyeliner,
>>>or lipstick,
>>nothing,
>just Annie, her grubbies,
>>and in every other way, naked, free...

She imagines Kelly driving her SUV, racing into a night endless with possibilities. She imagines Lake Pulaski becoming smaller, ever smaller, with each passing mile, the city lights and their dull orange glow diminishing. She imagines Joe moving home, starting over. She imagines Frank and his blissfully empty memory, which given recent events is pure gift. She even imagines Tom relaxed, Tom at peace, Tom swimming, swimming, effortlessly swimming.

The portal glows. She picks up a highlight pencil, leans forward, looks again. "Someday." She thinks. "Right now, there's so much that must be fixed."

Chapter 38

BRETT ON CHANNEL 10 SAYS it will be crisp and moonless, a perfect gazing night. Next to the pit, Joe drops an armload of firewood. In the center of the charred ring, he wads several sheets of newspaper over which he builds a kindling teepee. He strikes a match. A corner of the paper catches. A yellow semicircle forms. With a white puff, the paper melts, then disappears beneath the teepee. Smoke becomes flame. Joe adds more kindling, followed by a firewood teepee that he builds above the first.

Jen walks down from the house and joins him. By this time, day is yielding; red fills the western horizon, darkness fills the east. These two surround the remaining daylight, and advance. Red deepens, meets darkness. Venus rises. A star appears. Another. Another. Another. The protective dome vanishes as its pale blue limits and comforting illusion that "day light reveals all" surrenders. Like a flower, the night and its endless, sparkling pedals blossom.

Jen hands him a beer. The fire dies. Joe erects another teepee. Flames jump. In silence they sit and watch everything change.

Joe nods upward. "It is so improbable," he says. "They say it began 13.7 billion years ago, a speck so tiny it could not be seen with the naked eye. 13.7 billion years ago, a single thing that was, in every sense of the word, perfect. An infinite amount of stuff packed into infinite density and all the energy in the universe holding it together. It was a single thing, placid in appearance yet volatile beyond comprehension. Boggles the mind.

"Then something happens. What? Who the hell knows? Something. Something that, in an instant, turns those infinitely cohesive forces outward and sends a universe of perfectly packed stuff hurling away from itself. From benign to unspeakably violent, from an invisible dot to everything that is, the whole business comes unglued. Before that moment there is nothing, at least nothing anyone would recognize as being something. There are no galaxies, no stars, no planets. There is not even space. It all exists inside that little dot. After that moment? All hell breaks loose. Perfect order becomes total chaos. Space, time, exploding gasses scatter, become an endless river of stars and swirling clouds of vapor and dust. Gathering. Shattering. Planets and solar systems form, collide, reform. Red giants and supernovas erupt...and all of it, every last bit of it, races away from everything else at two million five hundred thousand miles per hour. What's more," Joe says, "is that it's still happening. The whole damned thing is still flying apart."

Flames fill the pit and lick its edges creating a rainbow, red, yellow, blue. The two of them watch fire do its work; wood becoming gas; embers becoming ash; heat releasing things as they are and changing those things, making them something else, letting go of what is.

Regret.

Blame.

The way things should be, whatever the hell that means.

Into the night, the fire rises dissipates, scatters, and in that moment creates a light and a heat that draws the two of them close to its source.

"That's enough." Joe thinks. He reaches out and warms his hands, "With a universe flying apart, what more could anyone expect."

The shrinking wood shifts and falls into itself. Sparks jump, cool, become nothing. A flame rekindles, rises, and for the briefest of moments takes its rightful place, the sparkling center of the night. It reaches up, flickers again, dies.

"Small," Jen says, "Everything is small."

"Yeah..."

"...Yeah."

The End.

About the Author

DAVID GRINDBERG is a Lutheran pastor, college instructor, husband, father of four, grandfather, pheasant hunter, scuba diver, and writer. For the last thirty years, he has been producing a steady stream of sermons, meditations, and articles. *Rapture of the Deep* is his first major secular fiction project and is published by Indian-Grass Books. A native Iowan, Dave and his wife Jill live in Fort Dodge, Iowa. You can visit him at www.davidgrindberg.com

CPSIA information can be obtained
at www.ICGtesting.com
Printed in the USA
FFOW01n1318220714
6452FF